About the Author

Hester Poppy Blenkiron lives in Yate on the outskirts of Bristol in the UK. When she isn't writing you can find her gazing up into space looking for new ideas for books. Doughnuts and coffee fuel her writing process.

Living Stone Island

H.P. Blenkiron

Living Stone Island

Olympia Publishers
London

www.olympiapublishers.com
OLYMPIA PAPERBACK EDITION

A CIP catalogue record for this title is
available from the British Library.

ISBN: 978-1-78830-988-2

This is a work of fiction.
Names, characters, places and incidents originate from the writer's
imagination. Any resemblance to actual persons, living or dead, is
purely coincidental.

First Published in 2021

Olympia Publishers
Tallis House
2 Tallis Street
London
EC4Y 0AB

Printed in Great Britain

Dedication

This book is dedicated to my mother, who thankfully is nothing like anyone depicted in this story, she's actually much, much worse.

"Even in the midst of fierce flames the Golden Lotus may be planted, the five elements compounded and transposed, and put to new use. When that is done, be which you please, Buddha or Immortal."

Acknowledgements

A huge thank you to Olympia publishers for taking me on with my first novel, to my friends, who I stole parts of their personalities from for many of the characters, and lastly a massive thank you to You, the reader, I hope you like my story.

Prologue

Can I ask you a question? Or better yet can you answer some of my questions? What would you do if every inch of your being told you to run away from life, to pursue a different path to the norm, and have nothing ordinary about you anymore? Can you tell me if this is an okay thing to do, if it is selfish, or wrong?

My story will leave these questions unanswered. But I promise, with all my heart, that it is a very good story.

Millie Darden: An Introduction

It started in October, as (in my opinion) all good things do. The winds picked up, the jumpers came out and the bastard squirrels had taken all the hazelnuts. Out in my mother's garden a frog looked up at me; grey and innocent. Maybe he knew where the nuts had been hidden away. Rake in hand, I smiled at it. Then the bugs stopped and hid, this meant rain was coming. I stopped too and smelt the air, acidic.

I have always been a rather lonely person. I figured my personality was an acquired taste, not everyone likes peaches after all, and they are of course, delicious. The frogs, crows and hares have always been there for me though. So has the wind, rivers, mud, stones and countless bonfires. The natural world is the best listener I've come across. It never judges or mocks. Also, it can be cruel and astonishingly beautiful all at the same time.

Yes, the land has always been there for me, like a friend who is good enough to teach you as well as love you. So when the land started to speak to me, I was hardly surprised. I think anyone can do it really, you just have to listen. It can start with a double take on a gusty day. 'Take the coast path, not the road'. What? Really? Fine. It can be as simple as waiting for the trees to fall so you know where the shed should be. Nothing about it makes me feel special, indeed, I feel like this could possibly be the norm and it's everyone else that needs to feel weird. For as long as I can remember I have always felt somewhat uncomfortable and unwelcome anywhere falsely heated or cooled made with bricks with false laughter and people who wear ludicrous things like pant suits and crew neck jackets. Ugh, I'm tensing up just thinking about it. No, I'd much rather feel the bitter cold or sticky heat that nature intended. Wearing practical clothing and a genuine smile, thank you very much.

As the rain started to draw nearer I retreated into the house. Costly printed leaflets and brochures from the local library adorned the kitchen table. I was nearing the end of adolescence and now was (apparently) the time when I and many others were supposed to surely know what we wanted to do with our lives. Hahaha. It all seemed quite silly to me. 'What pretend career shall I pursue in order to get my pretend tokens to pay for things that no one really needs?' Didn't medieval times have it making better sense? Swap a chicken for the seeds? Lovely. All the same, it was deemed rude not to at least *consider* one. I picked an apprenticeship in forestry in the end. It had the word forest in it, must be okay. Very good logic at that age, or so I had thought at the time.

'Forestry' turned out to be a small group of us in some underfunded college surrounded by sheep (good) but every lesson insisted on being inside away from the sheep (baa-aad). It became clear that you had to endure 3 years of sitting in front of a computer labelling Latin names of trees and making power point presentations to be good at forestry. I was most unimpressed to say the least. But, I did try. I even learnt to drive in the hopes that I could transport myself easily to the future job in forestry and maybe even live a sort of happyish life following all the rules and everything. It hurt my heart every time I filled up or paid money so that more tarmac could smother the land I loved so much. But this seemed to be the only way to do it and be acceptable to society. So I did — it was like trying to wade into a slimy bog that kept spitting me back out, it gobbled everyone else up quite happily but was never satisfied with my taste. I think the bog knew my heart wasn't in it.

Still, I had help, little nods of nature that kept me on my toes, an unlikely step ahead in fact. I felt that pressure and electric spark of the heavens. Big storm, hrmmm the roads will flood, college will be closed.

One more day to work on that essay, and a lie in. Soon it wasn't just nudges about the weather helping me out, after about a year things got even more interesting.

I started to get premonitions, sort of flashes of the future. When this happened it could be that I was simply sat on the loo, doing the washing up or talking to someone. But other times I would have grand scale dreams of paths I would take or should avoid. Once or twice the 'flashes' would not be for me but someone else entirely, I would have to creatively lie on the spot (not my forte) to complete strangers. One time I think I made the poor binman piss himself when I asked if he wouldn't mind just chit-chatting to me for a while whilst I practically had to use the wheelie bin as a barricade to stop him from walking under the scaffold boards that were going to crash down upon his very shiny head. Worst part is no one is ever grateful. They just think you're barmy. Like I said, perhaps they all just happen to hate the acquired taste.

I know, I know. No one likes the person who can't stop spouting on about how 'gifted' they are or how they're an 'indigo chilllld', but I promise I'm not one of those. In fact, I detest any notion of that kind of tomfoolery. I had more than enough helpings of crystal healing, guardian angels and seances from mum when I was growing up. My god did she eat that stuff up. Never ever shutting up about how I should, 'ask the universe' for food on the table, not her. Can you tell that I'm bitter? Oopsie.

Then something slightly more, well, off-putting started to happen. I noticed, of all the things, that I hadn't been pooped on in a while. Now hear me out, this is the bird in the sky kind of pooping not the sexual deviant kind of pooping, just to clarify. As someone who spends an inordinate amount of time outdoors, one can't help but notice that nature… just does have to go sometimes, and sometimes it lands on you, bummer, so what right? Some stupid fucks even think it's lucky. But it weirded me out that it hadn't happened for ages. Not just that but I hadn't even accidentally stepped in badger guff or cat shit either. Nor had I gotten debris in my eyes on windy days, no puddle got me, no thorn had pierced my skin. Bit of a lame super power, but hey, it was better than a poke in the eye with a sharp stick. Come to think of it that never happened to me any more either.

These things kept, well, not happening and the 'flashes' kept on coming until one night I was on my bike, riding back through the undergrowth of British B roads back home. I always rode on clear, full moon nights after I sold my poor excuse for a car, the best light to ride by. Back then bike lights were shockingly bad as LEDs weren't really around. At the time 'home' was living as a very unwanted guest at mum's place (she got irritated at my existence when I was around 11 and never really recovered). I mostly just sofa-surfed for as long as I could get away with and returned to do my laundry by night and be off by the morning. As you can probably tell by now the dislike was mutual.

Anyway there I was cycling by the moon light, like the flower child I was, when I heard a grunt. A loud grunt. All instinct should have told me to skiddadle, but I slowed. In a sort of trance, I stopped. Local legend said that there was supposedly a massive black panther on the loose in the area, so some say it used to be a pet and got too big for the owner to love it anymore and was 'set free'. Ever since, farmers have sworn that their chicken massacres are the work of 'the beast', not poor-quality fencing and hungry foxes.

A rustle came from the hedgerow, and slowly, with all the grace of a Japanese forest spirit, an adult buck stepped out into the potholed-ridden road. I froze. Was he pissed off? I felt so intimidated, 'this must be what it feels like to be mugged', I thought. He cocked his head upwards a touch with a soft exhalation of breath. Good he wasn't pissed off. I slowly stepped out of my bike frame, the squeak of the brake didn't alarm him at all. This creature was showing some serious sass. Suddenly, as if it were the animal communicating, I knew he wanted me to follow him. I left my bike against the edge of hedge, I knew it would be fine, and followed the fallow through the track he had made in the brush from countless journeys through.

Once on the other side of the hedge I followed him along the edge of a mostly barren field, it was autumn after all, only about half a mile later I began to hear the local river nearby, the night time trickle echoing off the overcrowded ash and hazels that grew alongside it, all the while my new friend silently walked onwards. We walked with the river until the woods drew near, he never looked back at me before jumping at a slightly narrow point in the river, frightened of losing him (what if he started running?) I went to wade through without looking only to find the rocks there as if perfectly placed for my feet. Nice. I could get used to this kind of treatment from mother nature.

Another twenty minutes or so of woodland and we were in what looked like a round coppice clearing, about ten foot wide. Evidence of a charred bonfire lay in the middle of the circle, the moon was directly above the area of cleared trees. It was astonishingly beautiful. It had grown colder and I could see the buck's breath shoot out of his nose like an exhaust, as we both stood at the edge of the pit. I didn't shiver at the cold. But what I saw next made me; all around us, slightly out of the light of the moon, were different sized shadows. More creatures. I took a minute step back. It couldn't be an attack. Far too magical to be an attack, I hoped.

First I saw a fox, then a buzzard, out of the gloom more and more animals kept approaching; badgers, a heron, a vast quantity of toads. The toads did add an element of safety to the whole thing. If I was going to be attacked surely there wouldn't be toads present. We'd always gotten on so well. After one or two minutes I could count over twenty animals there in the clearing, none quite breaching the middle. All in formation, almost like they expected a speech.

The buck turned to me and blinked. I felt my eyes roll to the back of my head, a soft, cushiony, falling feeling engulfed me. I felt as though my whole body was tipping mid-air, whilst pulsating. Like I had been in a very expensive massage chair for slightly too long, and I had lost all feeling of where my limbs were. This sensation lasted an unknown amount of time. Then time skipped and jumped, like it does in dreams and all of a sudden I was standing upright again. But somewhere completely different.

This was a hard place to define. Even with my best efforts. It was akin to a lighter, pure form of where I had just been, but at the same time it felt as though I was in a memory. Everything was lucid and unattached. Impressions of the circle of trees were there, I could see my own hands, that was a good sign. The light was strange, almost as if I were underwater; each colour tinted with the same brush. I realised I could hear things, beautiful natural sounds, birds and wind rustling grasses. Looking to the centre of the pit, now void of the animals, there was an orb where the bonfire had been. It was hovering slightly above the ground and was iridescent like a soap bubble, turning slowly in a hypnotic way. The orb made me feel safe, just looking at it made me realise all my troubles meant nothing, for the universe was so vast, how could anything be truly good or bad? Everything just was, and that was just fine.

I had approached it without noticing. I felt as if just staring at it wasn't enough, I needed to touch it. My right hand reached out without me telling it to. As my fingers felt the surface, the orb imploded. A warm electric shock rocketed through my body; first up my arm then building up in my chest, shooting down my stomach to my legs and feet, it overwhelmed me and entirely consumed me. We were one now and forever. I felt the sheer force of nature within me. A scorching fire, a reckless wind, the crushing oceans and the formidable earth. I was different now. A new violent light within me.

My spirit had grown, had been stretched and moulded into something entirely different. The earth had chosen to give me a gift. Somehow even then I think I knew it was a test. Time flickered again. I had to return. I closed my eyes willingly this time, knowing what was to come. My body pulsed, I felt the now familiar feeling of rolling backwards mid-air, my stomach lurched and I was plunged into icy cold air at top speed. Then nothing.

I awoke lying flat on the forest floor. A light frost had covered me and the surrounding dead leaves. An entirely pink sky was above me, day break. I was shattered. I picked myself up and looked at my surroundings; I was still in the circle of trees, the fire in the middle was still barren, the fauna however, were all but gone. I felt, well like I'd just spent the night sleeping on a forest floor, but otherwise, well. Perhaps a little disorientated, but well. I held my right hand up, the only difference about me appeared to be a most peculiar pattern coming from my right index finger. Where I had first touched the orb, funnily enough. It looked cool. How can I lie? It was like lightning down my finger on the back and front of my hand, I stretched my sleeve down, it faded down to my elbow. I'd always wanted a tattoo, but when my money came in, spare bike parts and food always seemed to gobble it all up, I was sensible, my priorities were in check. I wouldn't spend disposable income I didn't have. This was free and far nicer I decided. Win, win. I felt troubled by nothing. Sure I'd had a surreal out-of-body experience, but on the plus side it looked as if it was going to be a gorgeous day, best get on with it.

I took one last look at the pit, brushed the leaves off my backside, and stomped off. My bike was still where I had left it.

Leaving

Everybody's parents are different. Some get smothered by their parents, some get the perfect amount of love from them, others get taken away from their parents they're so bad. My experience was mixed, but altogether, on the whole, quite unpleasant to say the least.

My mother and father met in America, my mother was on holiday whilst my father was over for work. He worked (and still does work) for a large company that makes aeroplanes. Dull as ditchwater job, he did something to do with human resources back then I think, but he wasn't short of money. My mother was a self-employed spiritual medium, if you can call that a job. They (I'm told) hit it off immediately at some bar, and mum was quite convinced he was the one from the very off.

They both didn't live very far from another once back in old blighty and continued to see each other for around two and a half years. It only came about that mum wasn't the only woman in his life about a year into the relationship. I remember Dad saying he was surprised that she wanted to still see him after finding out she was the 'other' woman. Dad then got the guilts and tried to break it off, his other lady Catia (who he had married 9 years prior to seeing mum) had, surprise, surprise, noticed he hardly ever came home at night and did the sums. Dad says Catia was upset but wanted marriage counselling and for him to stop cheating, rather than a divorce. Dad obliged, but upon breaking the news to my mother she was beside herself with grief (this is one of the only parts of the story that lines up with both of their sorry tales of woe). In a bid to make dad stay I'm guessing they must have had a bash at it because nine months later, the precious miracle that is I, was born.

Dad says she told him she was on the pill. Mum says they both made a decision to have me to try and repair their relationship. Either way, my conception was undoubtedly unwanted by both of them by the time I was born. To quote my farther, 'She just got so angry, the minute you were born, she wouldn't tell me why. She was never the same again'. Perhaps because she realised 'the one' didn't want the child she bore to keep him and wasn't going to stick around out of a sense of duty either. Just a theory. Either way, pretty piss-poor decision making on her behalf. Terrible adultery and consequences of adultery for him.

Growing up with this situation was rubbish. Yes, I had a roof over my head and a room to call my own-ish (Mum used it as a storage space too), no I didn't actually starve, though I was terribly underweight for a good portion of it. Weekends at dad's place (a haughty old manor house in a tiny Cotswold stone village) were quiet. I never felt welcome, not with dad's wife Catia looking at me like I was the spawn of Satan come to take all her share of the money away when dad died. My father's attitude to parenting didn't go further then bringing the weekend bag up to my room on Fridays, mailing mum a cheque, and driving me back to mum's Sunday nights. I mostly took the opportunity to eat, being a large couple they always had good nosh stacked to the rafters.

Mum was slightly different and everything was (sort of) normal until I turned 11. Also the same time that her boyfriend of 5 years, Jeff, left her overnight, giving no reason. The bloke just legged it. I have reason to believe that she thought it my fault.

Jeff hadn't wanted kids either, she was at least sensible enough this time to get an abortion. He didn't come back. Neither did my old mum. From then on I wasn't allowed out for two years apart from to go to school. My social skills suffered. I started to have a complex about being outside. She stopped doing my laundry, caring for me when I was ill or had nits, stopped making dentist and doctor appointments, and the food I was 'allowed to eat' seemed to keep dwindling. She disliked the mere sight of me and I had to be in my room most of the time to stop her cataclysmic rages. Eventually I turned thirteen (the earliest age you could work back then) and as I had secured myself part-time work (at the local hotel as a cleaner) and she didn't want to make the four-mile drive to pick me up on weekends, I got a bike. A heavy, oversized, barely working piece of junk, but a bike none the less. This changed my life. I stopped seeing dad on the weekends to fit in more shifts, he couldn't of cared less, same old. Not only could I now afford to buy some more food (I got very savvy at buying at 'price per calorie' as I needed all the energy I could get) I could go out and see my school mates and do loner kid things like play curby till two in the morning and start smoking. She saw how happy this made me and started to comment on how 'out of control' I had become. She stopped paying for the school bus annually so I had to ride to school as well. What with school, my buddies (a rag-tag group of unwanted kids, who were out as late as me), and my job being four miles away in the next town over I started cycling an average of sixteen miles a day. Go to school, come back, get dressed, eat, go see people/work then home at around nine or ten at night to do coursework.

This suited mum, she never saw me. I got used to it after a year or so. I got strong. I started to notice my legs and arms as trim and buff. The strength on the outside made me strong on the inside. All of a sudden I shouted back. I got in her face if she got in mine. If she banged a table to make me scared while she shouted, I banged back and broke the fucking thing. I stopped doing her household cleaning for her. I used as little as I could physically get away with from that house so she had nothing to get a hold of me for any more.

We lived like this for years. Then I got something else. Something deep within my core in the woods on the way home one night. It was time.

***

"What are you doing up so early?" She's so high and mighty with me, this is mum otherwise known as Lucy Knacksaw (thank god she gave me dad's name; Darden)

"I slept in the woods." True.

"Don't be ridiculous, Millie. Also it's now the second of the month, I haven't seen your rent yet."

"That's because I'm not going to be staying here any longer."

"Yes okay, I want it by the end of the week. Other people don't have such relaxed parents you know."

"You won't get the money. I am leaving. Now. Today." I've found talking to her in simple easy to digest sentences is critical to me not losing my rag and hitting her. At this point I'm rummaging around trying to find my survival book that I read on the loo and my old hiking backpack in the storage cupboard/my room, trying desperately to enjoy the calm before the storm.

She tries tack one; horrible false niceness, "Please Millie, now look; you can't just up and go. Where are you going to live? You don't even have a car any more, be sensible."

"I'm leaving." Calm, detached.

There was a split-second pause before, "DON'T BESOFUCKING STUPID. You are a tiny, blonde, female. If you go it alone out there someone's going to rape you and you'll have nowhere else to go because guess what, I WON'T TAKE YOU BACK IN!" Tack two; fear.

"I'm still leaving." Mild boredom.

Then came the howling anger infused with great helpings of crazy eye, "HOWCANYOUDOTHISTOME! AFTER I RAISED

YOU SINGLEHANDEDLY, YOU KNOW I DESPERATELY NEED THE MONEY, WHO ELSE CAN I RENT THAT ROOM TO? IT'S TOO SMALL NOONE WILL FUCKING LOOK TWICE! YOU ARE ABANDONING YOUR ONLY FAMILY, YADDA YORDY YOO I'M SUCH A MASSIVE BITCH BLAGH BLAGH BURRGH..."

Okay so that last bit was just my memory failing me, but you get the idea. She's mental. The whole back and forth went on for a hour or two with me calmly collecting my possessions or anything useful of hers I felt entitled to (matches, loo roll, bin bags, etc). I knew I'd have to rough it, for god knows how long, hell I didn't really have a plan. I was going on a hunch, something told me my gut was to be relied upon a little more these days after the forest incident too. Anything I had to carry with me had to physically be on my back or in my panniers on my bike. So far my itinerary consisted of:

- All my dried food high calorie energy bars, oat cakes, some quick noodles and the like
- All my tinned and canned food (I hate beans AND tuna but convenience beats taste this time)
- One almost full jar of peanut butter and a huge hunk of cheese
- Multi tool, comes with handy fork attachment, beloved and used almost every day, anyway
- Pocket knife and blade sharpener
- Plastic bags
- Bin bags
- Loo roll
- Small survival book (filled with useful bits about what herbs and berries you can eat, and how to skin rabbits. That

sort of thing)
- Rechargeable torch that doubles as bike light (another worthwhile purchase, batteries are expensive, my legs keep going for free…pretty much)
- Socks, underwear and one spare sports bra (you forget what normal bras feel like when you have to cycle everywhere all the time)
- Moderately priced waterproof gear (my first big purchase since the car, worth every penny)
- Thermals
- Hiking water bottle
- Tampons (I rarely got my period any more, but you know what happens when you don't bring any)
- Toothbrush, paste, hair and shower gel combo, one (thin) towel
- Thermal sleeping bag
- Two massive, heavy-duty square pieces of tarpaulin with ring holes (this will be my shelter and the heaviest thing I carry)
- Rope, around ten metres
- Hair brush
- Lip balm
- Lighters and matches (I was good at making a fire but hadn't fully mastered flinting yet, I'm not Bear Grylls)
- Small first aid kit
- Puncture repair kit
- Hat, fabric headband, and gloves
- Spare clothes
- A new-found confidence not even Lucy could tarnish.

I could hear my mother silently having a massive strop in her room, all tuckered out. I'd filled the hiking backpack properly with all the weighty objects near the back part. I found myself taking a last look at my box, sorry, my room. The garden, overrun with bindweed (my mother insisted she liked it but always complained when it engulfed her veg), the Ikea kitchen, the various spiritual knick-knacks, dotted around. The lack of any photos of anyone but herself in one old Polaroid by her desk; she was smoking a cigarette and looked about twenty. I stared at her wide face and mottled brown hair. Back when I was little, and things weren't quite so pear-shaped, she used to joke that she'd picked me up in Norway as a souvenir. I had a large forehead, Nordic cheekbones and white blonde hair with big blue eyes. Looking at my wide, brown hair and hazel eyed parents I suppose anyone would think I wasn't theirs. Then I recalled how in later years she'd started to resent my looks. Especially my hair. She used it against me when I tried to leave the house sometimes, 'You can't go out on Friday nights sweet, the bad men always go for the floozy blonde. Do yourself a favour and dye it brown, you look like such a show-off.' Or she'd say, 'Aren't you worried people won't take you seriously? If you want to get anywhere in life that hair is not your friend.' I never understood why my peers cooed longingly at my eye and hair combo. It never seemed to do me favours, girls hated me before I'd even opened my mouth and guys seemed to think it meant I would fuck on the first date without fail. Most wouldn't even get past the blonde jokes before moving on. My hair colour made me appear empty and vapid to the rest of society. Why in the world would anyone want it? The main reason I stopped dying it was that I didn't have free rule over what I could do in mum's bathroom ("dye it, but not in this house!" Nutter.) and dying it in other people's homes breeches the weird line no one ever speaks about.

I even had a cheeky cup of tea before departing, this was a safe bet as her super strops usually lasted a few days, so a twenty minute cuppa was fine. I put my key on the side, thought rather than said 'goodbye', unlocked my bike, adjusted the gear and was off.

Nomadic Existence

As I rode a thought that perhaps I should say farewell to the odd cluster of people I usually hung around with occurred to me. Hrm, three miles in the wrong direction and a great deal of waiting for them to all finish various shifts and head to the pub, it still being around nine in the morning. It didn't seem entirely worth it. It just wasn't the kind of group that would miss me all that much. We clung to each other out of survival instinct, safety in numbers and all that, and for someone to get pissed with usually. It never went further than that. Pretending it did just wasn't my style. A small flash of awkward hugs and annoying questions showed anyway, but I'd already decided before the handy hint of the promotion.

Already I was noticing the subtle changes I could make on the world around me; the wind was somehow always with me when I was riding. This can sometimes be a ten mile per hour advantage. No complaints there. I had no idea where to go really, apart from a vague notion that I wanted to be around the hills, but larger hills than home provided. Anyone else would say heading north when winter was just around the corner was very stupid indeed. Pah, I knew better. Hills had running water (usually), tree cover (hard to build housing estates on the mountains) and lots of wildlife to keep me company (and well-fed if necessary).

The day was turning out to be quite a pleasant one, the sun shone, but not too much so that I had road glare to deal with, the wind kept me going and even the traffic wasn't proving to be too tyrannical today. By midday I had crossed over the large river that headed out to sea and was in a different country to which I had started in. The brilliant progress meant a well-deserved lunch, whilst riding I thought about the cans in my rucksack, but being this close to civilisation still I felt I could probably take advantage of consumerist greed.

I was right; a little way inland I entered a town, busy and rife with midday mum shoppers with prams. Perfect. Little 'trying to be modern' cafes with poor excuses for al fresco dining out front, were everywhere. All I had to do was fill a plastic bag with their leftovers yet to be cleaned off the tables. Confident as anything I calmly shut three of the little Styrofoam parcels and put them in my bags as if I was eating to go, hopped back on my bike and was eating some little shit's chicken nuggets that he'd taken one bite out of on a park bench next to a pleasing duck pond. I'd clocked a small supermarket down the road too, midday throw outs of the yesterday's pastries should be soon. There was a drinking water fountain ahead of me to fill my bottle up. This was easier than I thought. It seemed I had unknowingly had years of practice for this kind of living just being under my mother's (mostly metaphorical) roof.

Dustbin diving, food and drink pinching and occasional shop lifting were some of the things that had kept me going when minimum wage for teenagers wouldn't suffice. Some of the people I'd now call 'my old friends' taught me the best ways to steal. Self-checkouts are your friends for one. Mega calorie packs of cookies and doughnuts became one banana with an oopsie daisy attitude. Coats with inside pockets are very handy. Always do it on the busiest days. If caught always be calm and collected, anger and fright just make people have more of a power trip when they've got you and they're more likely to call the police than if you swallow your pride and grovel nicely. All little handy hints for the unwanted children to pass along, to help us survive our parents.

I waited like a hawk just out of sight of the back double doors of the supermarket, and sure enough, some sort of morph-look-alike, acne blob, came out and dumped the food bags right on top of the growing pile (I even knew which ones were fresh! Awesome). I side jumped the gate easily and grabbed one of the two bags. In and out in under twenty seconds. Too easy. I took what I could carry (stale muffins, a few gingerbread men, two Danish buns and a sausage roll) the ducks got the rest. Lucky bastards.

Don't get me wrong, it's not always this nice, or easy. Once when I was around sixteen, I got too greedy and kept up the same spot for weeks, one of the store employees must have cottoned on but decided to take matters into their own hands instead of telling the boss. Instead of a bolt lock on the gates I found a steaming human shit in one of the bags. Lesson learnt, and what a waste of slightly off bananas.

I found a good spot to stop for the day after around four hours more cycling. With no bed to rest in I didn't want to overdo it too much, weakness in the wild can be more serious than when you've a roof over your head. Plus, I needed the rest of the daylight to set up camp. Look at me sounding all Steve Irwin. I wasn't quite so elegant sounding when I was trying to get my bike over the bloody barbed wire fencing earlier in the day.

I picked a spot well off the beaten track, I'd last seen a public footpath about a mile ago, there was a good chance I was on somebody's land, like always, but I hadn't been shot yet so I figured it was a good as spot as any. I was on quite a slant with a rocky outcrop all around me, tall evergreen trees stood close together and plentiful. I started with my "roof sheet" looping the rope I'd brought through the metal holes, I first tied it to one tree beyond the rocks and one in front, so that I'd made a wide and low upside-down 'v' shape. My ground sheet came up against the rocks about a quarter of a metre up and then was held down on the ground with stones and sticks through its own metal holes, sort of makeshift tent pegs. It had to be up against the hill just in case of a flash flood, at least I would have some sort of cold icy warning before my possessions floated down the hill/ river I'd decided to camp in. I really hoped it wasn't a dry river bed. A small survey of the area confirmed no. Lovely.

Once set up I feverishly changed into my thermals, not cycling makes you cold. I trusted my bag to the woods and left my new home for the night in search of wood (the wooden kind, boyfriends weren't my top priority at the moment), I didn't want to draw attention to myself but all the same I hadn't brought any books or laptop with me (I'd never owned one in the first place, useless expensive toys, can't even drop them in the bath, pah) and I needed something to do in the fading light. The forest provided and I soon found the debris of an old tree fallen amongst its comrades. As the forest was so tightly packed, when a tree fell here almost all of its branches came off neatly in the process, clever design see. The wood was light and dry, it would burn hot and quick, as it wasn't freezing temperatures yet this was perfect for my needs, I gathered three large bags full, and headed back, picking up dry spindles and grasses along the way to help with ignition.

I was almost out of wood and contemplating forced sleep when I heard a familiar scuffle. Somewhere to my left was a creature, I knew what it wanted; it had smelt the trail of its favourite kind of slug down here and was mildly wondering if the bright spot was safe to go to. I poked my head out at it from the tarp and said 'Boo!', the young badger looked up at me and blinked slowly. It didn't seem remotely bothered and carried on sniffing and scuffling until it had found the slug, as it ate it glanced at me a number of times. I reached for a gingerbread man and ate alongside the creature. This counted as a house-warming party I decided. After a while, others joined us, they must have heard about the great slugs I had to offer party guests. Seven badgers and one human. What a night, surprised no one called the pigs. Such a raucous shindig was had. They snuffed around me (being mostly nocturnal creatures) until I nodded off. All jokes aside I felt quite protected. It was genuinely comforting. They didn't even eat my stale pastries.

Over the next few weeks, I developed a sort of pattern, to get me through the days. I would wake at first light, pack my things and transport myself and my bike over whichever fields, marshes or woodland I had ended up in the night before until I found a road. The wind, forever on my side blew east, so I found I rode mostly east too. When I came across towns or lone petrol stations I would stop and eat, raiding bins or pilfering when I saw the opportunity. I'd love to tell you I gathered blackberries and nuts from nature's kitchen, but the truth is, this takes an awful lot of time to gather a substantial amount, and is tiring in itself to do. With no certainties ahead of me, greedy humans leave the most food, and I took what I could get.

After eating and a short rest I would find a source of water to drink from, I would drink till I felt I would burst and fill up my bottle and several others I had acquired along the way. I would then have what I'd always called a 'whore's wash' in a sink; just face, pits and crotch. Unless I'd found a gym in the town this was the best it got, or rather, the cleanest I got, till I came across fast flowing rivers (the cleanest water) where I could have a proper cleanse (provided I had established no one would be looking). When good clean water was nearby, I found I always knew, like I had a homing device inbuilt for it or something. I felt similar to the kind of auto pilot your body goes into when you're walking home or to your local shop, you don't really have to think about it, you just somehow find yourself there. I would then keep on riding till the sun was about two or three hours away from setting and find a camp. Wash my clothes if a river was close, gather firewood and have dinner. Sleep. Repeat.

At times I would think of my mother. Did she miss me? Had I done the right thing? What had she told others had happened to me? I wondered why I didn't remotely miss her, more, I missed the childhood and mother that could have been. I was missing a past that never happened. Other times I would think of the future, what was I doing? Sometimes doubt would creep in, and I would find myself panicking that this was me forever. Just constantly moving, getting grubbier and grubbier until one day I'd turn into mud and no one would even remember who I was.

These thoughts didn't last long, I found whenever I felt some sort of negative emotion with my journey, be it the cold, the wet, the lack of fresh foods, or the aching muscles from so much cycling, a little nod of hope from the world around me would happen. Once I was crying with frustration on the side of the road. It was pissing it down with icy rain. I had to deal with the second flat tyre of the morning and my hands were so cold I couldn't fit the inner tube back with much success. I banged my fists on the sodden ground like a toddler. So angry at myself, I'd done this a thousand times before, why the fuck was I struggling so much now? Then out of the corner of my eye I saw a squiggle. To everyone else, that's a squirrel. I've always called them that since I was kid. I couldn't pronounce the fine enunciation required to say the word 'squirrel' back then, so they've been squiggles ever since.

The squiggle clocked its head at me, almost in sympathy. With lightning quick movements, it gradually came closer. My amazement stopped my tears, and I reached out my hand. The squiggle sniffed me, decided I was okay and then seemingly out of nowhere produced a hazelnut and gently placed it on my palm. I closed my fingers around it and said, "Thank you". I realised these were the first actual words I'd spoken in a long time. Not only that, but I was talking to a squirrel. I found myself smiling. I gave myself a break and set up camp early that day. I fixed my bike by the warmth of my fire (fire was somehow never an issue as well, I'd always been quite good at making them, but never before had I been able to ignite wet leaves). In the morning a neat pile of hazel nuts stood in a cluster in the middle of my tarp. I counted seventy-seven. I broke several of them open with my trusty multi-tool and saved the rest for later.

Sometimes the people I encountered on my travels were rich in their kindness. A dirty face and haggard clothing make some people give you money or the other half of the sandwich in their hand. These people are the ones that make the earth a pleasant place to live in. Some people however weren't all that nice. There's no jokey way of saying it; Some people want to hurt you.

So far, I had witnessed myself take control of the wind, have a second sense about water and inhuman abilities with fire. One moonless night I discovered I could physically move the earth beneath my feet, or rather someone else's. I had a spout of bad luck and couldn't find some place hidden in the countryside by night fall sometime in early November. I could smell frost in the air. Shit. I'd spent an hour too long in the comfort of a cafe nursing a rare coffee, brought with the change I'd accumulated from looking like a bum. Now it was dark and I was miles from the safety of the wilderness. I hurried around this bigger than I expected market town, the roads were like a maze and I kept looping on myself without realising. They were so badly drawn out that I got confused and nearly went headlong into a bus. Over tired and grouchy, I looked for signs for the nearest park, to hell with it, that would have to do for tonight.

The town's local park was big but flat. Flatness is never ideal as there are far fewer places to hide. But to its credit it had a makeshift 'woodland' at one end. I couldn't help but think the inside of the fake woods was quite cool, well for kids anyway. Not super sophisticated grown-ups like me. I could see my younger self thinking of it as the best thing ever. It had a wooden castle with turrets and everything, with chain-link wooden plank bridges coming off it at all different heights. These led on to different assault course type activities, the tyres embedded into the woodchip, monkey bars and one solitary horizontal pole...for hanging off perhaps? Who knew the thinking of town council park planners? Not I. This was all encompassed within the woodland bit of the park. The castle looked just about big enough for one shortish person to call home, or at least bed, for the night. I stepped towards it, then a stillness caught the back of my head. I was being watched. Fear trickled down my spine. I thought of my knife, at the bottom of a tightly packed side pocket in my rucksack. Hardly quick access. I'd felt so invincible in the past few weeks that I'd forgotten that some people are actually bigger and stronger than me. I turned around, a tall dark figure stood about ten metres away. Shit, shit, shit.

"Are you lost sweet'arrt?" There was a hint of a smirk in the sentence, he and I both knew he wasn't being nice.

"I have pepper spray, my dad's expecting me home, I live about two minutes away mate. Nice try." I inwardly applauded myself on my quick thinking and forced bravery in my voice. I did wish I had had the foresight to bring a phone or at least a phone-like object to pretend to call someone with.

"I don't think so missy, I think you're lying, didn't Daddy ever tell you not to lie?"

"I really don't have the time for this, sod off."

"I saw you in the cafe and sat on the street, begging for food. You're pathetic. You're a little homeless bitch." Fuck, he'd followed me. Fear now choked me. "Why don't you come with me? I'll look after you." He had started honing in on me, like a wolf hunting its prey.

"I'm alright thanks." I could barely talk. The street lights were too far away to see his face.

"We can do this the 'ard way, or the easy way, sweetness. I don't want to 'urt you more than I 'ave to" another big grin at the end of his sentence. I now felt profoundly sick. He took a big step forward.

"DON'T." I wished my word sounded fiercer, listening to my own fear made it all the worse.

"Yeah, what the fuck are you gunna do?" He went to take my throat with his hand, I pushed my bike at him and crouched low on the ground, there was no time to scream before I felt him grab my ankle and pull hard. I was dragged across the ground towards him. So much adrenaline and panic pulsed through me, suddenly the fear was gone, ready to fight I turned and grabbed his face with both my hands and used my thumbs to press as hard as I could into his eye sockets. He let out a bark of pain, my bike still on top of him he had to untangle himself before he could get a hold of my wrists, he pushed my bike off himself and tried to pull me off. My strength had increased, I even felt bigger than him as I pushed down even harder, I felt the ground suddenly tremble around us, then a huge crack like a tree splitting in two came from beneath him; the ground had opened up around his huge body and was rapidly being caved in, the ground was swallowing him under my command. I knew if I kept pushing and let the energy flow freely through me, he would be completely submerged and die. A part of me said serves him right, what's to stop him from doing this to someone else, this will end him and his sadistic ways for good. Another said this might just put him off for life anyway. I pulled myself away just in time for his head to be the only thing left above ground. His eyes (what was left of them) were a bloody, mangled mess, I had blinded him. I had won. I had moved the earth so that it ate him up. I looked down upon my hands dripping red. I was mildly glad that I hadn't killed him.

He was screaming, it sounded as if it were underwater to me. I was dazed with my own power. I spat on him, picked up my bike and left.

The Boat

After that encounter I stayed well away from civilisation, not that I was scared, no, I just didn't want to bury and blind any more people than I really needed to. One morning I was making my way up a steep slope to find that at the top there was the faint smell of sea water in the air, and that wideness you can sense. Sort of like your brain can perceive the vast ocean ahead even though you can't actually see it. I was surrounded by vegetation, trees and brambles, but I was sure the sea was only five or six miles away. I looked up. A gull. I smiled. Still not quite sure of where my final destination was or why my instincts were taking me this far out, I decided not to worry about it, I was well into the swing of things now, may as well keep going.

An hour later of following gulls and ocean smells and a small stream myself and my bike were at the top of a cliff, I'd reached the end of the land, a beautiful expanse was beyond me. The sea, the sea. I threw my cycle down and spread my arms wide embracing the wind and the spray. The sun dazzled me when it came out from a previously very overcast day. It was like a beacon; 'you made it'! Roarrrr, and the crowd goes wild! I did this silent scream whisper to myself repeatedly; 'Arghhhhh, yeahhhhh woooooo', whilst simultaneously shaking my clenched fists in the air, doing my best imitation of Muhammed Ali when he won that famous boxing match.

"I don't know about this, she seems pretty weird.". I jumped a mile. Who the—

"Yeah, but everyone deals with it differently, don't be so

harsh to judge." Two women had somehow creeped behind me, totally silent, and were apparently watching me celebrate my coastal milestone. They looked similar to me, a bit bedraggled and dirty, like they too had been travelling for a long time in the wilderness. The one who spoke first was shorter than the second and had a face like a slapped arse, with a jet-black bob haircut. The other was taller than me with flaming red hair, and a definitely kinder look about her.

"Why is she just staring?" said slapped-arse face.

"To be fair we're staring at her too." said nice redhead. I coughed awkwardly, they both realised I was human, but continued to stand both with their arms folded like I was something annoying they had to look after. The wind picked up around us forcing us all to stand a bit closer together.

"Er, can I hel—"

"I'm Robyn, and this is Grace," the redhead pointed to her sour-faced partner, Grace gave me an eye roll and a half-wave of her hand with her arms still folded.

"We've come to collect you." Grace mumbled.

"That's great but I don't really need collecting thanks." I didn't take a step back, though I thought about it.

"Here we go," scoffed Grace.

"Just give her a minute, we haven't explained anything yet."

"We've been waiting here for two days, it's our last day of the full moon can we just go already? Why does this have to always be such a bloody drag. I say we knock her out, take her to the island, then explain, it would be much quicker than this touchy-feely nonsense Kit has us doing every time."

They both then started a quiet but furious argument over the way to go about 'collecting me'. I took the opportunity to slowly grab my bike and make it down the 'steps' of the cliff to the beach below. I had no idea what they were on about but I sure as hell didn't want to be knocked out and taken to an unknown island. No one wants that. But the earth wasn't having it as I tried to make my escape. The natural 'steps' I had chosen that moment, started to crumble away beneath my feet, my bike hit my hip as it crashed 30 feet below me, bouncing off part of the cliff just for effect.

I held onto the sea grasses lining the edge of our cliff and as I pulled my weight and scrambled up the grasses got longer and thicker with each pull intertwining themselves around my wrists for better support. Handy. Once standing both the women who went by Grace and Robyn were staring at me again, their argument halted by what should have been awe, or shock or anything other than what they showed on their faces; which was mild disappointment. "Oh dear, well I suppose that will do for now. You'll get training when we get there though so don't worry." Robyn said sympathetically.

"Who says I'm going?" I said breathlessly, still holding onto the grasses.

"We do, idiot."

"That's not nice, Grace." Robyn was clearly the leader of the situation. "Now look," she continued, "Gus over there's already got your belongings in the boat, it's about an hour's journey, if you hate it we'll send you right back and you can be on your way. But you'd be the first, well, the first in a long time anyway." There was indeed an old, haggard-looking man with dreadlocks plonking my bike with its panniers full of camping gear into a tiny wooden boat on the shore line.

"So you're saying I should just get on some random boat with three people I've never met before to go to an island I've never even heard of...to do what exactly?" I was getting a bit pissy and defensive at this point. They weren't doing a very good job of explaining themselves.

"All will be explained by Kit when we get there, promise." Robyn was being very casual, like it didn't matter, but I had a sneaking suspicion that it did matter. A lot.

"Do you think we should go get some more supplies while she dithers about?" exclaimed Grace, huffily.

"What supplies?"

"It's not all about you, you know, we've got other things to worry about besides your fragile ego."

"GRACE!"

"What? It's not as if we're going to murder her, she needs to chill out. We've got stuff to do."

"Whatever, but I want a snack, I'm starving." I held my hand out for Robyn to grasp, to show solidarity after my rudeness.

"Excellent! Off we pop then!" Robyn was pleased, and yanked me up in one movement. None had even asked my name yet and I was going on their boat. I amazed myself. They did have my bike after all. I didn't like my chances of wrestling it off the big and scary Gus.

***

On the boat we were all quiet. In the awkwardness I noticed bag upon bag of shopping filled with rice and pasta and tinned food. I ate my apple, (the first vitamins in god knows how long) and surveyed our vessel. I noticed one big problem. No engine, no noise. How was this thing running? Then I saw; Gus had one hand outstretched towards the water in a relaxed reach, almost as if he was about to pet a dog, his arm had the same swirling, inky marks as mine now had. The water moved as he moved his hand. He was moving us. Moving the water around us. Gus gave me a wrinkled, fisherman's wink, then smiled, his skin like leather at the corners of his mouth. Robyn and grace continued to look ahead, unfazed by this. They were unfazed about what I could do too, what was this place we were headed to? I attempted conversation, "So, uh, I got the impression back there you didn't want to wait around for me too much, are we in a hurry for something?"

"As a matter of fact, yes," Grace continued to look ahead while she spoke.

"We didn't mean to rush you, but, well you were a little late. We need the full moon to get across the water, poor old Gus here has seen better days and he needs all the help he can get." Robyn smiled as she said this, Gus simply nodded in agreement.

"How can I be late? I didn't even plan to be here?"

"Urgh, it is so frustrating when they don't know any of it yet. Look, just trust us okay? We were told you'd be here two days ago, you're here now so let's just get a move on." I wasn't sure if Grace and I were going to get on. Robyn reminded me of a worn-out mother the way she reacted to her.

"Look we aren't really allowed to say a great deal about this to you just yet, but do you see something familiar about our hands?" Robyn rolled up her sleeve and held her left hand outstretched, Grace turned and did the same, finally enthusiastic. I held my right arm out too. All four of us had the same markings down from a finger, cascading round eventually to our elbows or thereabouts. I noticed mine went the furthest. "See? We're all the same. You're going somewhere where people like us can learn more."

"Hold it sugar, you'll ruin the suspense," Grace smirked wickedly. Her mark on her hand looked the most imposing against her dark skin. I was a little jealous. It was hard to gauge their ages, but at a guess, Grace looked perhaps a year or so younger than me and Robyn had four or five years on me. Gus looked about one hundred and two. Grace's confidence made her seem older though, whilst Robyn's kindness gave her more youth.

All around us fish leaped out of the choppy sea, wiggling their tails as if marching us forward. This made me feel a little more content, creatures always making me feel more at home than people. In the distance I started to see a small grey lump on the horizon, as we got closer Gus gave out an ear-piercing whistle in a fairly complicated tune. Robyn looked at me apprehensively, 'It's time.'

The Island

Upon arriving at the shore line of what I only knew as 'The Island' I felt a queer sense of my body jolting as if we'd entered some sort of bubble. I couldn't physically see anything odd or peculiar but I felt different. Very different. Like I was connected to the others, somehow. Grace looked on me with different eyes and said, "Oh Millie, maybe you're not such a prissy madam after all," whilst she unloaded the shopping bags full of food, with that same enigmatic smirk of hers. I did a double take, her knowing my name, shocked me more than Gus powering the boat forward. Why was I not so 'prissy' now all of sudden, did she know something? I thought 'screw her' I wasn't 'prissy' before! I took in my new surroundings; classical landscape of home, but with a richer variety of trees and other plants about the place. The shingle beach led up to a grassy hill where the trees were all almost bare of leaves, was it December yet? Perhaps. A strange formation of steps came down to where we were and I followed the others up to the top wheeling my bike along with me, and lifting it up each half-metre long step, my only familiar. The island couldn't have been more than two miles across.

We came to the top of the steps, it was getting darker now and spitting with a light rain, gulls swooped in and out of my vision. I noticed fairy lights strung along a willow archway. Pretty. The girls and Gus waited, whilst I stood behind them. As if on cue, a very tall and stately looking woman (well, she would have looked stately if she wasn't wearing warm winter clothes), she was the kind of woman who you could imagine being in a renaissance painting, possibly of royal blood. She looked about mid-forties and had a long pale face and a thin nose with brownish hair pulled into what must have once been a neat bun on the top of her head, but now had lots of straggly bits coming off of it, "Oh well done girls, well done for persevering, so sorry about the wait, this one's been harder to track than most, why don't you put those bags in the kitchen area and have a break for the rest of the day hrm? No dinner duty for you two, now off, off you go! I have Millie to attend to. Thank you as always Gus." Grace stomped off without a word and Robyn gave a small wave and a brave smile my way. Gus made a motion with his hands at the stately woman and I realised he was using sign language. That explained his lack of words. The woman signed something quick back and he took my bike. "Don't worry petal, Gus'll just take that somewhere dry for you for the moment," I immediately trusted her, like she used to be my nanny or something, just being in her presence made me feel at ease. Something told me not to push her though. There was definitely something fierce beneath the sweet.

"What is this place?" I was trying to rack my brains to remember whether this island was on any map I'd read before.

"Good afternoon to you too, Millie! What a wonderful present your presence is!"

"Oh, uh, sorry, hey."

"No matter, no matter, you made it in time and that's what counts."

"You're, you're Kit!" I said, surprised at myself, the name had just sort of arrived in my head.

"Oh fabulous, nice to have a quick learner every once in a while, the girls showed me your maneouver at the beach, how you used the grasses to your advantage, but I know you can do more than that so don't let them put you down about it, not for one second."

"They…showed you?"

"Yes dear, in their minds." She paused to look me up and down, held out her hand for mine and I obliged. I saw her raise her eyebrows quickly at the length of my mark, then recover herself. "Let's just go for a quick wander down the beach shall we, explaining all this in front of everyone isn't necessary, I find people take the news best one on one, come."

We walked down the wonky stairs, and just hearing the waves again calmed me even more. Kit cleared her throat, "So, this is never an easy conversation. But I'll do my best to answer all your questions as precisely and as punctually as I can. Is there anywhere you'd like to start? Or shall I just ramble on dear?"

"Well, I guess the main thing I'm wondering about currently is… is how on earth Grace knew my name, but it was like, she only knew it when we got here, to the island."

"Ha! Most people ask about the guardian's mark first! Aren't you a little trendsetter? Well, Grace knew your name, Millie, Millie Darden that is, because as soon as you arrived within the island's limits you and herself and everyone else in that shoddy old boat of Gus's became connected to what we call the 'hive mind' of the island. You see this in other creatures a lot, starlings and bees and an awful lot of fish use the ability to have a hive mind in order to work as one. It's really very efficient. Us lot on the island all have the ability to connect with one another in that way, as there are so many of us here at any given time the effect spreads and makes communication that much easier for us. It works with fewer people too, but the effects just aren't quite the same as when we're all together. Of course if there's anything you'd like to keep to yourself I'd recommend flexing your brain muscles a bit."

"So it's like telepathy?"

"Yes and no, we can communicate feelings of joy or danger or when we need help, and anything in between. We can also show each other memories, that becomes very handy. But not actual sentences and conversation. Best to think of it as emotional communication rather than straight up telepathy. But you're not all wrong. As you saw Grace got your name, this was likely because you yourself were inwardly wondering why no one had asked for your name, so it was right there in your head for the taking, see? Grace has always been particularly good at the hive mind game though, the clever little sausage." Kit was coming across like a proud headmistress of some fancy private school.

"Well yes, I suppose it is a bit like a school, which brings me to our next topic—' I really would need to 'flex my brain muscles'. Here you can learn to control and expand your new skills in the safety and protection of the island. There's no better place than Living Stone to hone your powers, as I always say!" She put emphasis on the words 'Stone' and 'hone'.

"So that's the name of this place? Living Stone Island?"

"Yes, yes, I inherited it off of my grandfather when he passed, oh, how many years ago now I don't recall. That's why it's not on any map you see, it's private. If anyone comes here that isn't personally invited by myself they will pay a sorry price. Especially if it's to get at my students." She suddenly burned with rage for a fraction of a second, I thought I had something come through to my mind but it was wiped away before I got to see. I was betting Kit had some seriously strong brain muscles. "But no one really calls it that, if you want to fit in just call it the 'island' dear." I nodded.

"You said 'my students', so is this like a school? For people like me?"

"Right and wrong again my sweet. You will learn here but it is by no means a school, just a safe haven really. I just call them my students for a lark really, hah hah! You can leave whenever you like, but I do strongly advise you to stay until you've at least got the basics. Things can get dangerous out there if you yourself don't even know how to control what you've now got within you. All I ask is that if you are staying, to help out with cooking dinner, clearing the place up together etcetera etcetera. You'll learn all about the task board when we go up for dinner, I'm sure the others can fill you in on that sort of thing Now, I expect you're wondering about what exactly you'll be learning in the first place, eh?" I nodded again. "Yes, well, as I know you've noticed you have some degree of control over wind, water, fire and earth. These are the four elements. You can progress with each in different ways. Some students find they excel in just one element and some find they have moderate proficiency in all. Everybody is differently abled and I will not bow down to people who think they are better than others, do I make myself clear?"

"Yes Kit," I didn't mind the army sergeant tone, my excitement was mounting rapidly.

"Lovely, now let's see…anything essential I may have forgotten. Ah yes! What animal was it that took you?"

"Excuse me?"

"The animal, the an-i-mal dear that took you! Pretty much everyone here has a similar story of how they gained their powers. Most involve some sort of creatures taking them on what in my studies can only be described as a trance-like journey. I'm still trying to figure out what this all means in the bigger picture. You do remember how it happened, don't you? Stop blocking me! My word you learn fast! Amazing!"

"Oh, I'm sorry! I wasn't trying to block you I swear! Drat. Keep on her good side goddammit. "Uh well, I was on my bike and this male deer with huge antlers had me follow it, but then we got to this other place and there were all sorts of other creatures there, did you want the one that led me or all the others?"

"Hrm, were the other's land, water and air dwelling creatures?"

"Yes."

"What of fire, was there a fire anywhere?"

"Yes, yes there was in the middle of the area I was in."

"Hrm yes, very interesting. You'll be one to watch Millie. All four elements for you then. Of course it goes without saying that a condition of staying here is that you must try with myself and the others to figure out what all this means. I'm a woman of science, so when this first happened to me I was very sceptical, haha, oh what a laugh, I thought I'd accidentally taken acid. The very thought! But hrm, yes, are you with us? Will you stay?" I looked her in the eye, then back to the mainland. I thought of my mother, my rag-tag group of drinking buddies, my home.

"Yes. I'd like to."

"Spectacular, so glad I didn't put you off. I think it's goulash for dinner tonight!" she exclaimed as she wrapped her long arm around me and led us back up the pathway.

Greetings

As myself and Kit came to the top grassy mound of Living Stone Island, I heard laughter and the crackle of a large bonfire. Through the lit up willow archway was an open area surrounded with logs and stumps and what looked like homemade wooden chairs, though they had a much more natural look about them, as though they had been grown into the shape of a seat. I suspected that was exactly the case. There were about thirty or so people of all different ages and backgrounds gathered around. Many small creatures and birds lingered on the floor and in the trees, comfortable to be there as pets. A small selection of people were huddled together speaking what sounded like mandarin. There were some older groups too with bellowing laughter emitting from them who all had mugs clutched between their hands, and a smattering of children between the ages of six to early teens leaping about playing some sort of game that the objective appeared to be who could annoy the others most with either wind blown into their ears, small sparks in their faces, or mud clods thrown like snowballs at each other, all using their power to playfully annoy. Some of the older looking people were lighting cigarettes with a quick swish of their hands in a lazy movement. I was astonished at how normal they all looked. Take away the inexplicable magic and you'd think you were at some sort of child-friendly eco-festival.

Kit held me by the arms standing behind me and said in a loud, and authoritative voice, "Everybody, this is Millie, our new student, she's got here by bike, no less, and is probably very tired, and well, she is a bit damp too, so make some room by the fire and please make her feel welcome." With a little push from behind, Kit was gone. I saw Grace and Robyn sitting together, both looked sideways at me, still unsure. I felt myself swallow hard and walked over.

"So, Kit says there's a task board I should be checking out?"

"Yes! Of course, we'll get to that but first please help yourself to some stew." Robyn grabbed a metal bowl from a pile nearby and ladled me out some delicious smelling concoction and handed it to me. "You're lucky there's any left, those kids nearly demolished the lot."

"Exquisite cuisine as always BinBin!" cheered a slightly older, sizable male, lifting his empty bowl in appreciation.

"Yeah, you'd know Lardo," said Grace, in little more than a whisper.

"Say what you like my love, and as loud as you care to, we all know what you're thinking anyway," replied Lardo with a laugh. I had felt it too, but also the chemistry between them and the jealousy of his compliment to Robyn. This was going to be intense. Was every single social situation going to be so laid out and transparent?

"Oh no, hun don't worry, you'll learn how to block out all their nonsense soon enough. You'll be able to turn it on and off like a FM radio don't worry." Robyn winked as she said this. I wolfed my goulash down, it was glorious to have some proper sustenance, it warmed me and made me feel slightly less anxious about the whole thing. "Wow quick eater, let's get to it then! Come on Grace, you can show her the ropes with me. Grace looked grateful to get out of the fire pit, but gave Lardo a flirty poke in the neck as she passed him.

The three of us walked around the pit and down another willow tunnel (I was starting to sense a theme here) into another area that had a very large and rustic log cabin in it. It had a pleasant decking area with three or four washing-up sinks and cupboards lining the sides and walls, above the sinks was a gigantic chalk board with evidence of much rubbing out and hastily made changes to a big chalked out graph with what must have been everyone's names all down one side and various jobs down another. I saw that in new chalk at the very bottom someone had already written my name and assigned me to: AM: LESSONS and PM: BUNKS. Other tasks said things like DINNER and VEG PATCH ASST.

"Aww that's nice of Kit, looks like she's put as all in the same schedule for tomorrow," Robyn gave my arm a small punch.

"Urgh I bet we get Grayson for lessons though, he's such a melodramatic bore. He never lets us do anything that might tarnish our inner ethics." Grace made quotation marks around the words inner ethics. I got an image of Grace lying flat on her back with rocks rapidly forming around her wrists, presumably as some sort of punishment, the image then flicked to Robyn frantically patting down another girl's hair that was on fire, and What must have been Grayson yelling at Grace. Robyn raised her eyebrows at me as if to say, 'There's a reason he's so strict with Grace.' Grace then retorted with, "She was asking for it. Who cares more about their hair than their ability to defend themselves anyway? Served her right. Set her straight. I do these things because I care too much you know."

"Well, I'm sure Millie will make up her own mind on that debate. There's a loungey area the other side of the cooking and washing up base, but we try to only use it when the weather's really dire. Let's show you the bunks for now, there's no set place where we all sleep, but we sort of order ourselves by age and boys' bunks and girls' bunks. Luckily, we've got several handy workmen who've got powers here too, their job never changes from 'maintenance' on the board."

"Yeah, maintenance may as well mean sit around smoking

and saw a piece of wood every ten minutes to them though."

"That's not true, Angela pulls her weight." Robyn wagged a finger at grace.

"Yeah, I suppose she does bring a slightly more girly element to our surroundings too, without her it'd look like a bloody tsunami had hit."

"And there'd be no fairy lights. Or willow arches."

"Or snoring." I surprised myself when I chipped in in the banter. It was well received and simultaneously impressed them both.

"You'll give Grace a run for her money with that kind of mind skill," smiled Robyn.

They must have seen my image of Kit saying then same thing, as then Grace popped up, "All right all right! Freaking show off."

At the bottom of the next pathway the opening was much bigger, it looked to be around seven 'bunks' that looked largely similar to the cooking lodge only with more windows, and wellies untidily lobbed onto their individual porches. "You can sleep in the end one with us, we had it all to ourselves but I think you'd probably prefer that than sleeping alongside the kids," exclaimed Robyn. We walked to the end cabin and inside was very simplistic; ten single beds with plain covers lined the sides of the walls with a small window every so often and dull, single bulb lights above each bed. A small wood burner stood at the furthest end. It was reminiscent of army bunks or American summer camp's sleeping quarters I'd seen on T.V. Robyn explained the shower block was just around the corner and that if I wanted to be clean to best start the day early.

***

We found my bike and belongings and brought them into the bunk. Once changed and washed I built up the courage to ask them a few more questions, as I still felt very much in the dark about what exactly the arrangement there was, "So how did this place, you know, the island, come about? What started it all?" I had tried to sound casual, but my burning curiosity shined through.

Grace leaned in from her bunk and spoke in a mock horror story voice, "We can only drink the blood of the innocent, we need newbies to feed our unquenchable thirst for power."

"Don't be so ridiculous, you were new here too once Grace and you had twice as many questions as Millie," sighed Robyn, brushing her hair.

"Come off it, I was only playing."

"As you've probably guessed, Kit's the founder. The story goes that she was a scientist working on the mainland and she discovered she had some degree of control over the earth and of water. Being a very logical person, she tried to find out the cause, but had no luck. She inherited the island shortly after discovering there were more people like her—"

"But how did she know? How did she find them?" I interrupted.

"We think it must have been similar to how we all came here, some sort of hive mind trace draws you here, it draws us to one another like an instinct, like we're a pack." Robyn continued. "Because there was already more than one of us living here, more and more kept arriving, people were drawn to the sheer numbers we think. But it's all guess work. Kit is still trying to figure this all out. Yeah she often jokes that she wishes more people with PHDs were gifted, like we're not good enough or something."

"That's definitely not what she means by that Grace, think of it from her point of view, it must be frustrating, having all these people here, just as confused as she is, all of us expecting her to figure this out just like that." Robyn clicked her fingers to emphasise her point.

I looked to the floor for some time drinking in all this new information. I wondered how they each came here, were their experiences the same as mine? I jumped as Robyn said, "Yes actually very similar! Let's have a look—" Robyn focused on me for a second and I showed her my encounter with the buck in the woods. "Oh, wow, that's very much like mine! I was walking down the street after finishing up at the cafe, where I used to work, when all of a sudden, this fox started following me. It was so friendly, then it led the way up to this giant hill, although the locals will call it a mountain. I fell into a trance like you and when I woke up, I had this brand new 'thing' on my arm and I knew I had to come here, like a homing instinct. I do miss my family though, I'm sure they're worried sick." Robyn finished off with a guilty tone in her voice. Then looked to Grace.

"Yeah, well some of us already knew we could do stuff, even before the vision." Grace's expression grew dark. "I found out I could affect the world around me when I was attacked by my stepdad. He'd just broken my arm, same old angry fit after the pub on a Friday night. Mum was out, but she wouldn't have cared less. I was so pissed off and hurting I didn't even realise his lighter had exploded in his hand as he lit a cigarette, catching on the alcohol content in his mouth. I just stood and watched as the flames got bigger and bigger. But I must be a saint as I had the decency after a while to drench him with water. I ran outside and a black horse was just bloody standing there, outside my door, like he'd been invited over or something. I followed it to the big lake nearby and hey presto, mangled arm got healed in the vision and I had a nice-looking tattoo to top it off. I came here and the rest is history."

I could tell Grace wasn't the type to want too much sympathy, so I left her story there. "So what happens if, you know, the government found out? Is that why she chose the island? To keep us all safe?"

"Well think about it numb nuts, we can't just go gallivanting about around normal people and just be like, 'oh don't mind me, just carving a small tunnel underground with my mind so I can get to work on time and beat the traffic', people would notice and freak out. When people are scared of something they don't understand they usually try to attack or kill whoever's scaring them." Grace got quieter toward the end of her sentence and touched her arm subconsciously.

Robyn quickly picked up the conversation again, "It's safer here for all of us, that's why, everyone, well, almost everyone, chooses to stay. Including yourself." I had a sudden image in my head of a tall, surly looking man from Robyn and got the impression there was a story they weren't telling me.

I delved deeper, "Who chose not to stay? Why would they?" Grace and Robyn exchanged looks.

Robyn spoke, "Well, there was one guy people talk about, supposedly was one of the very first people to have powers along with Kit, was with her from the very beginning, even before the island was set up. He, well, it's all rumours and here-say, and stories get exaggerated, but apparently he was kind of... well-"

"Evil."

"No Grace! He was just misguided, thought he could do

better without Kit, they say he thought we should be using what he had to change the world, not hiding away, like we're ashamed of what we are." There was silence for a brief moment.

I asked, "So where is he now? Becoming batman or something?"

Grace did a bark of a laugh, "Ha! Most likely, no one's heard from him in years, he could be an ice cream man by now for all we know."

"That's the dream," Robyn laughed.

First Lesson

I did as Robyn asked and woke early. There were already several people loitering around the shower blocks, having conversations with mouths full of toothpaste. An angry looking man with a forehead like a Victorian radiator came over to me and introduced himself as 'Mr Grayson', I had to try very hard not to show the image of Grace setting that girls hair on fire. "Your classes start in about half an hour, just follow the little ones and you'll find the practice area." He gave me a thumbs up and turned around to continue his toothpasty conversation. The showers were surprisingly warm and I found that I was liking the whole 'joint' bathroom thing. Always nice to brush your teeth next to someone, for some reason, to share a small ridiculous moment in life. Us humans we get foamy mouths every morning and night and it's very normal. Very normal indeed. The girl was sharing this moment which looked to be one of the ones who was speaking another language last night. She had short spiky hair. She paused for a moment beside me and gestured me to look her in the eye using her fingers in a 'v' shape between the both of us. I complied. I had the oddest sensation of a loud voice in my head speaking mandarin, although I could inwardly hear the foreign dialect she was using, I could somehow perfectly understand it. She said 'Hello, my name is Chunhua, nice to meet you." She laughed at my gaping foamy mouth. Then pointed at me, I cottoned on, looked her square in the eye and focused. I tried to say "Hello my name is Millie, nice to meet you too," but I had a flat feeling in my gut, I knew it hadn't worked. Chunhua cupped her ear as if to say she couldn't hear me, then said in my head, still in mandarin, "Don't try so hard, let it come naturally, like breathing, don't even think about it." Once again, I looked, and took a deep breath, trying to let it happen without effort. Chunhua suddenly gave a big smile and gave me a small, cutesy clap, then spat out her toothpaste and waved goodbye. I had just introduced myself in mandarin through my mind. I decided that no matter how badly other things might go that day, I should still count it as a success. It was strange that Kit only thought the hive mind could convey memories and emotion, wasn't she supposed to be the brains around here? Why would Chunhua keep something like that from her? I let it slip from my mind easily, there was still so much I didn't know about this place, I figured all would be revealed in due course.

Once dressed, I walked through the willow arches to where I could hear most people talking, I didn't get far though as I found myself in a queue. It looked like breakfast was coming in the form of a production line of bacon rolls being handed out as people passed by the kitchen area. I felt my stomach yearn for food and took mine gratefully from a woman with long, frizzy hair and wearing big round sunglasses for the bright day. I had the name 'Angela' in my head, she winked and then vocally said 'Next!' I was pleased everyone seemed to be being so helpful. But was keen to do my fair share of jobs come the afternoon. I hated being a taker and wanted to even the score already.

Halfway through my sandwich I found Grace and Robyn round the now dead firepit. "And what a surprise she's already done with breakfast. You have to be the quickest eater I've ever met young Millie," joked Robyn. My mouth was full so I just showed them both an image of Grayson telling me to follow the children with a comical amount of toothpaste dripping over his chin. We did indeed follow the children down the front steps to the beach. We walked awhile, everyone else knowing the journey, myself, still chewing. Eventually we got to a wider stretch of beach with a giant carved out 'room' inside the cliff edge. I wondered if this was natural or made by the people here.

Grayson turned around and divided us into two groups. He spoke with a clear voice, but it was taken away somewhat by the sea air around him, "As we have a new member here we're going to be practising some pretty rudimentary stuff today, I'd like the older and more experienced of us to please monitor the children among us as I do only have one pair of eyes. You lot with me, "He gestured to the group I was in with Grace, Robyn and a smattering of older people, "everyone else on water and air until I say swap, understand? I want no injuries or troublemaking today, let's all set a good example for Millie, shall we?" He looked at Grace in particular as we wandered off to the cliff side opening.

"Now I'd like to do earth first in here as we all warm up a bit, then we'll go onto the fire once we're all used to using what we've got within us. Pair up, Millie you're with me for today just so I know what you can do, then we can work from there and see what you need the most training on. Right, off you all go." Everybody teamed up as I walked over to Grayson. "Now then it's probably easier if you can show me what you've done in terms of shifting earth before, Kit's already told me that you are capable of doing all four elements, but you'll find that you're probably still stronger at some than others, for now anyway. Go on, don't be shy." I gave him the image of the man in the park being swallowed by the ground. There was happy chit chat and an excited buzz around the place before this, but everyone stopped. It appeared that I had not just sent this image to Grayson alone. Or had they all just been listening in?

"Holy cow, Millie, nice one!" Grace shouted in the silence. "Very impressive, but do remember that our powers show themselves when we are in the most danger. When adrenaline runs high so do our inner energies that carry this gift. Learning to control it is key.

Without control you could very well accidentally kill your best friend in an angry flash." Everyone was somewhat humbled and carried on in their own groups. I could see what Grace meant with this guy's ethical code, he seemed more afraid of the power than most too. There was probably good reason, I thought. Grayson returned to instructing me once everyone else once again appeared to be busy.

"Now I want you to first focus all your inner energy to your feet, stand tall and breathe deeply. That's it. Keep breathing and try to remember how you moved that earth over the man in the park, keep that feeling in your head, and hold it." We practised this technique several times until he was sure I had the hang of it. After a while I stopped hearing the clatter and talking of the rest of the group. Grayson then chose to communicate via the hive mind and told me to switch the energy to my hand and hold it outward. Grayson picked up a beach stone and placed it in my hand. All I could hear was my own heart beat after that. Then a small crumbling sound as the rock in my hand turned into sand as I clenched it. Somehow to me this seemed far more impressive than what I had done to the man in the park. This wasn't anger or fear forcing me to act, this was me calmly controlling the force within me. Sure it was only a small stone, but still. I was delighted.

After half an hour or so of crumbling the rocks Grayson gave to me me, with much success, we all gathered around in a circle ordered in what Grayson thought was most to least confident with fire skills. Grayson produced a small flame within his hand. He passed it around the circle starting with the kids, each person having to focus energy into the palm of their hand to a) stop the burning sensation fire tends to cause, and b) add some fuel and make the fire slightly bigger each time. I passed the test with ease, only catching my thumb on the flame by accident. Though I was a bit disappointed to have been lumped with the kids. By the time it had reached Grace it was quite large, about the size of a football, who then added about double what others had done and then passed it on to the last person, who happened to be Lardo. Lardo's beard had caught fire in his panic and someone shot a small jet of water from their hand to put it out. A long lecture from Grayson followed this. Lardo's eyes never leaving Grace afterwards, he seemed to truly enjoy her cheek.

After an hour or so it was time to swap groups, whilst Grayson was checking in with the other team to see how they'd gotten on, myself, Robyn and Grace gathered together, "Don't worry chick, we can teach you some cooler stuff after hours, it's like going over the alphabet every day with this chump." Grace pointed over her shoulder at the weary eyed Grayson. I was surprised to see Robyn smiled at this too, as she seemed to be so sensible.

"Yeah, we can finally test out this trio theory too seeing as we're all unified."

"Unified?"

"We, you, me and Grace, all have some control over all four elements! We call it being unified. It's rare!"

"Yup, the word is that Kit thinks unified people can combine their powers somehow, I personally cannot wait to test this. You in?" Grace gleamed at me with a mischievous look in her dark eyes. "Of course, but what's going to happen, how do we, um, unify, exactly?"

"I guess we'll hold hands and make daisy chains and see how we go after that. How should I know? It'll be fun to find out though."

"Kit said to me she thinks it's to do with the hive mind, we have to be on the same wavelength, both literally and figuratively first. After that, she's not sure either. All she said was that 'the power of three' is common in nature, so it would make sense that that was the reason why me and Grace were struggling before." Robyn shrugged her shoulders.

"Well, I can see that, a triangle is the strongest shape in nature after all, if that's what this all boils down to I won't be too surprised."

"Just be prepared for me to be *extremely* disappointed if nothing happens," said Grace, then she added, 'No pressure."

We walked to the sea line with our group, and Grayson told us we were all to practice holding back the tide. There was a chorus of groans from the group. After ten minutes I could see why. Holding back the tide was very draining, I could feel myself sweat on the spot as I focused all my body's energy reserves into my tiny area of tide. I had only managed to keep it at bay, a small seawater wall of about five inches stopped in front of me. Still better than half the group. It was similar to the feeling of holding many really heavy items that you know for sure you're about to drop and break all over the floor. Grayson explained to me that using power of water was like a muscle, the more you used it the stronger it got, so water training was really like going to the gym compared to earth, air and fire. I hated the gym. He told me to view it like building up strength on a bike, this made me feel marginally better about it. There was hope after all.

The last lesson was for air. Grayson got his 'star student' to do a demonstration. It was Chunhua, the girl from the bathroom this morning. She stepped out in front of the group and raised her arms, ballet style, above her head and closed her eyes. The younger girls of the group whispered excitedly, like this was a show they'd seen before. Chunhua slowly made the sand swirl around her in a graceful spiral, I was mesmerised. The act was so enchanting I forgot where I was for a moment. The sand suddenly was concentrated around her feet again and Chunhua slowly rose into the air, hands still raised, body still poker straight. She had the calm face of someone who meditates. Then out of the blue, Grayson threw a heavy looking driftwood branch at her, with a smile, confident she could take it out. Still a float, she waved one of her hands around her head and channelled the wind around her into blocking the branch and snapping it in two, also managing to shield the crowd from the debris. She came down from her height of about four feet in the air, and bowed with a small smile and rejoined the group, her friends all giving her praise in her own language.

Robyn whispered over to me, "She uses the sand too so we can all see what she's actually doing and where to direct the air flow, otherwise it'd be impossible to try and replicate it."

"Huh, clever." I replied, somewhat intimidated now by Chunhua's skills.

Grace heard my mind and said, "She's good, but she ain't unified hun. People with only one element in them tend to excel at it. We've got a bit of a disadvantage having to learn all four if you ask me. It's like being given three times the amount of homework that everyone else has to do..."

"Less gossip over there please ladies! Now pair up again!" I dutifully walked over to Grayson. This time he explained that learning about air was similar to skills used in meditation. Having to clear your mind completely and let go of everything in it. I had never tried meditation before, life was always so stressful and chaotic, to me sitting down and thinking of nothing just seemed like a giant waste of time. But I would have to learn if I wanted to progress with this element, apparently. I thought of the times I had some control over the wind, on my bike, free and thoughtless, unknowingly directing the breeze to push myself along. I stood beside Grayson and tried to replicate that feeling in my mind. Nothing. Grayson then tried a different approach and dropped some fallen leaves from the bracken behind us slowly over my hands, I made the smallest bubble of safety around my hands so the leaves didn't touch me, a big soggy one landed on me right at the end when I lost focus. Air was proving tricky. I saw Grace getting frustrated with this lesson too over my shoulder, grumpily getting twigs thrown at her by a laughing Robyn, who earlier had shown great skill in doing the sand swirling technique. Grayson explained that calm and collected people were always better at controlling air. Drat.

The last portion of the lessons was dedicated to a group meditation as the sun set. The other group re-joined us from the cave and sat calmly with their legs folded, hands on their knees. We followed suit. After five minutes or so everybody settled. I started to feel my body breathe in and out in time with the ocean before me. The breeze tickled my hair around my face, I didn't feel the wholesome emptiness that I was sure I was supposed to be feeling, but it was relaxing none the less. I felt in tune with my own body, sure of the power within. I thought briefly of my mother and whether I had made the right decision coming here. What was she doing right now? Probably making haphazard guesses at what some poor old biddy's late husband would want to say to her beyond the grave. She usually gave sweet and loving answers. I thought that perhaps what she did, even if it was faked, was still good for people. There was nothing wrong with having faith and hope after all.

Long after the sun was set, I turned around to find many people had left without me noticing, maybe I had been more successful than I thought. Grace was to my left and had a large frown across her face. The face of determination to be relaxed. Robyn looked to be on another planet all together. I got up and made Grace jump, "Oh, Christ alive, it's dark already, how long have we been here for? I never stay this long for this ponce stuff." She got a few, angry, one-eyed 'shhhhh's' from the few that remained.

Robyn looked me up and down, thinking, "Maybe there's more to this unified thing than we thought. I wonder if—"

"Yes, that's right it's time for dinner, off we go." Grace grabbed both our arms and lead the way around the beach, telling us both to "shut it" in her mind. We did.

Back at the cabin, after we had each grabbed a bowl of chilli that was going around to eat, Grace explained herself; "I'm not sure if we should be going around openly talking about this whole unified thing until we're sure of what it means." She had a very serious expression on, unlike her. "It's just that, it could mean more than we think, you know?" She shuffled on her bed, uncomfortable with her own words.

"You don't trust Kit?" I spoke in a matter-of-fact way, remembering Chunhua's blatant hive mind speech to me in the bathroom that morning, Grace wasn't the only one with trust issues concerning Kit.

"No. I don't. Not that I think she's a bad person, she just gives me the creeps sometimes. Like there's something we all don't know. She's always down in her lab, what does she even do down there? It's like she's keeping something from us."

"If that were the case then why is it that we can leave the island whenever we like? She's good to us Grace, she'd set this whole place up just for us, and other people like us. So we can learn about what it is that we can do. To me she's a godsend. Who cares if she does research all day? She's probably the only one right now that can figure this all out, we need her."

"Yeah, I get that, but she still weirds me out."

"I'm with Grace, I think she's got a point, no matter if we stay here or not, maybe we should keep schtum about this until we, the unified lot, find out a bit more. There might be nothing to it anyway. No big deal."

"Right! I agree. Sorry Binbin, looks like it's two against one." Grace was quick to jump on my agreement. Robyn shrugged her shoulders, going with the flow. We quickly and impatiently cleaned all the bunks, making beds and chucking sheets into the laundry room.

***

We'd decided on waiting until everyone had gone to bed. As the last cabin light went out we tiptoed out to a place further inland on the island. Robyn led the way with a torch, while Grace was behind me covering up our footprints in the mud, sweeping her hand across the earth every so often. We came to a place that looked like it had been an old base, smaller than the one used now with taller, older trees surrounding it. No sign of a fire in the middle. One torch was clearly not enough for the night, cloudy and with only a half-moon peeking out, every now and then. We decided lighting a fire together would be a logical and good start to us trying out our powers together. We all crouched down, our hands outstretched, and focused on the adrenaline needed to produce fire. Robyn suddenly paused and held her hands back, "Remember what Kit said? We have to be unified in our minds too. Let's all just check in to make sure." I heard both their voices inside saying 'check!' and replied accordingly. Already I felt like I had more energy. As if we all suddenly knew what to do we each held out a hand to the other, grabbing the place where we all had scarring down from our hands. Each with one hand free we concentrated on the spot in the middle of our small circle, and as if a gas canister had exploded, produced a roaring flame that had a shock wave like effect, rebounding outwards, shaking the trees around us. I felt my body hit hard on the floor of the wood. Then nothing.

Unified

As I woke, I realised I was no longer on the floor but in the air, maybe a foot or so, but still floating. In the same circle as before were Grace and Robyn, in identical positions to myself, clearly just woken up at the exact same time as myself. Robyn looked confused, possibly a bit scared, Grace looked like she'd been standing in a queue for half an hour. All around us was the familiar bright whiteness that had happened in my first trace with the animals. We were definitely still on the island, in the same clearing, but everything had a very pure and misty look about it. The fire we had just made still burning in the middle of us, silently.

Before I even had a chance to exchange looks with the girls, my buck was emerging from the woods around us, a fox and a gigantic horse joined too and stood beside them both. My buck nodded to me, Robyn's fox swished its large tail around her feet and Grace's horse nudged her on the shoulder. We all now looked at one another, unable to speak actual words, what could you say in a situation like this after all? The air around us seemed to thicken, I felt a heat in my chest, the orb that had gone in my chest the night of my trance was out again, right in front of me. I knew my stag was using its energy to keep me present, my whole life force was just there, glowing and slowly rotating, about the size of an apple. A blue-white light emitting from it. Grace and Robyn were in similar situations, the fox and the horse having thin strands of the blue white light keeping them both here too. Their orbs in front of their chests.

The balls of light started to spin faster, then rotated inward, still gaining speed. They were a blur for a second and then all three came together, adding mass to one another, becoming one big orb of a darker blue. Suddenly in the silent fire below came flashing images from within, like a distorted screen viewed from above water; Kit's regal face stained with rage, a stone shining in sunlight with some sort of engraving on it, a young man's face half-covered with a scarf, a clinical looking room with wires and machines everywhere, and finally a child falling, forever falling. So far down. I closed my eyes in horror. The now dark blue orb had split again into three and I felt it like a punch to the chest going back inside my body, gasping for huge gulps of air as I realised, I had been holding my breath, or perhaps, just unable to breathe the entire time it was gone.

I had the familiar falling sensation again, my whole body tipping back on itself, and the dizzy, nauseous feeling of a drunk. Falling forever backwards. The next thing I can remember is the bird song in the wet morning air, all three of us splayed out on the floor, still around our now extinguished fire. Bone tired and confused. Unified.

We trooped back to our cabin, it was only just day break so no one would be up just yet, we were safe. A silent agreement between all of us, not to speak of what happened to anyone. None of us liked the look on Kit's face that we saw in the fire. Grace had been right. That was certain. The whole thing had felt like a warning.

The weeks that followed were exciting and had a different feel about them. Myself, Grace and Robyn choosing to only team up together every now and then to avoid being found out. Our powers always amplified when together, to the point where we had to purposely fail a task that Grayson or the other teachers had set us just to seem like we were going along as usual. Our secret made our bond all the stronger, we were soon chatting casually between ourselves when we were other ends of the island too. For the first time in my life, I realised I had friends, true friends, not the kind that you just hang out with out of mutual pity.

The days were filled with lessons on the elements, I found I was learning at a fast rate, able to produce my own substantial fame in a matter of days, making roots arrive on request from the ground and even had some success with lifting myself with the wind around me and could easily conjure up a water wall within a week or two.

One day came, when the first buds of spring were forming on the trees and the birds were again chattery and active. Kit found me when I was off lessons, I was set to help with the sizeable vegetable patch on the task board. Spring was just around the corner so the now germinated seedlings had to be planted out for the meals to come. I was quite happily working alongside Angela, her teaching me about self-sufficiency and how before 'all this' she had her own allotment that was greatly missed. She showed me the more delicate side to using the power of the earth, how you could tend to a garden without so much as having to lift a fork when you had the power to move the ground in your own hands.

Kit came around the corner, I could feel her staring at me. I hadn't really seen her much since the day I arrived. I felt awkward. Like when your Gran knows you've forgotten her birthday. I felt her hand on my shoulder, not hearing her come up to me. She smiled wide, a warm feeling around her, then turned to Angela, "Angela I hope you don't mind me borrowing Millie for a little while, I need to speak with her." Angela shook her head of bouncy curls and smiled back in response. It was all very friendly, but I still felt like I was somehow in trouble. I blocked Kit and Angela before checking in with the girls who were down in the kitchens cooking for the day. Grace said they'd accidentally find me if I wasn't back in an hour, this reassured me somewhat. I walked with Kit.

"Is everything okay?" I asked.

"Yes, absolutely. I'm sorry you don't see much of me Millie, I think I do have a tendency to overwork myself, all cooped up in my quarters. That's what having a passion for answers will do to you though. My father was the same, I clearly inherited his work ethic." We walked a little further in silence, until I couldn't not ask another question.

"Where are we going exactly?"

"We're off to my residence on the island dear. I have something to show you, I think you'll find it most interesting." I kept my face impassive.

We rounded a corner and saw a small, stone-built cottage. There was ivy creeping up one side and it had rusty iron fencing all around it. It could have been an idyllic holiday spot, or a haunted house, depending on the light. Kit led the way to what looked like a cellar to the side of the cottage, opened the metal doors on the ground after typing in a combination, and hopped down to a ladder within with surprising agility for someone her age. I watched her head disappear and listened to the clunking sound her feet made on the metal ladder, and heard from what must have been quite far down, "Come on then! I haven't got all day!" Well then.

Once down, I realised how warm the breeze was above ground, down there it was freezing. I breathed out to see my own dragon's breath, but maybe I was a wuss as I didn't see any. Kit marched along turning on big buzzing lights all along this underground room. It was clear as soon as light flooded the area; this was the image we saw in the fire. The clinical room we had started to call it, on our many inward conversations about what those images might have meant. I was now sure, we saw glimpses of the future. I shuddered. The child falling echoed in my head.

"Welcome to my life's work. This is where I conduct my research, for the benefit of anyone afflicted with these powers." She said the word 'afflicted' like what we had was a curse. Kit strode around the room, proud. I saw jars of animals filled with fluid, in some only heads were present, and others were not quite grown and had a foetal look about them. The walls were lined with many graphs showing incomprehensible data, a world map on one side had pins of different colours in various places and names on them. I spotted mine, a black pin with a small label spelling 'Millie Darden' pinned precisely where I used to live with my mother. I kept my head clear. I could not afford to mess up here, with her, alone.

"I was wondering whether you could help me Millie?" Kit slowly strode towards me, hands behind her back. "You see, as I'm sure Robyn has told you, you are a very rare commodity, and have some control over all four elements. This is fantastic news for me. It would mean my progress with this case will skyrocket, if I can define what exactly separates you from people with only say, one or two or even three elemental powers. Now all I would need from you today is some blood samples and a quick scan—"

"Have you tested Grace and Robyn?"

"Hrm? Oh, don't let me make you nervous child, I simply chose you as you're currently the closest to my lab, you're not special at all. My time is everything to me." Kit scoffed as if I was a belligerent six-year-old. As stupid as I knew this was to go ahead with, I couldn't really find an excuse not to do the tests.

Kit took three blood samples from my arm, conducted an MRI scan (who knows how she managed to get a hold of one of those), and hooked me up to three different monitors while I had three Petri dishes in front of me; one filled with water, one with sand (so she knew I wasn't faking the air game I suppose), one with some match sticks and one with plain old mud. I did as I was told and showed power over all four elements whilst hooked up. I annoyed her when my matches broke so just produced a flame in my hand instead. Best not piss her off too much.

While she was taking the various wires out of my arms and legs, I noticed on her main desk stood a single photograph; a young boy with messy brown hair, darker skin than the woman holding his hand, both had 'we are taking a picture smiles', with stilted body language. The boy looked around ten years old, the woman holding his hand looked very familiar. I stupidly realised it must have been a younger Kit. She turned and saw me looking, through pursed lips she said, "My son, dead. I miss him every day." But her expression looked more curt, and angry, than sad. Mourning parents usually at least said the names of their deceased children. He may as well have been called 'Dead'.

She bustled me out after that with a quick, "Thank you, thank you." I returned to the vegetable plot, but on the way showed Grace and Robyn everything through our own separate hive mind.

Tragic Incident

The sun grew hotter as spring turned into early summer. More food was grown and harvested, and a richer variety of meals were presented to eat at the base camp. My skills of making what little we had last in the kitchen were no longer needed as salads, beetroot and peas started arriving on the plates. More fish were caught by Gus and the mood of the island was definitely better as less time was spent continually drying out sodden clothes from rain.

Our lessons changed too. Angela was taking more of a role in teaching. Turned out she had much more of an affinity with animals than Grayson. The whole group appreciated the change. Angela proved to be a much more relaxed teacher and laughter was often heard in lessons. She taught us that the hive mind can be extended to different groups of animals, reminding us that we were animals too, and that the separation of humans from our view of 'wildlife' was completely human-made. It was up to us to build bridges again.

The lessons first started with Angela performing a simple demonstration of the cruelty of nature.

She made her feet stamp and hoof on the, now dry, land and used her hive mind to conjure up an alarming amount of worms, beetles, ants, bees and flies all around her. It was neat to watch, but also a bit creepy. Once the bugs had formed into a very concentrated area at her command, she changed her mind to call for the birds instead; all manner of gulls, sparrows and buzzards appeared, some coming from way inland. Then again once the birds had all perched into the trees around the group, she gave a different kind of mind call, it felt earthier and richer than the insect and bird calls which were dimmer and more shrill than the latter. Mice, rabbits, voles and moles started coming from all sorts of crevices and holes in the ground I hadn't even noticed before. I felt like we were about to be ambushed there were so many creatures within the group, a sense of foreboding had arrived with so many different species in one place, all unprotected and vulnerable in the open space.

I felt it, and by the looks of everybody else so did they, when she cut off each individual call. Where there was still silence from the creatures before now there was a war. The birds screeched and crowed diving downwards. The small mammals scrabbled to eat the many bugs on the ground, and the flying insects flew wildly around our faces. In the frenzy the birds started swooping up the ground creatures, the larger animals fleeing back to their holes, safe due to their smaller cousins being easier prey. It took roughly thirty seconds for the chaos to come to an end. Very few creatures were left afterwards.

Some of the younger members of the group started to cry. People my age were shocked and quiet, the older members nodded with solemn wisdom. Finally, Angela spoke, "This is nature, at its most primitive form, our world has the unique ability to be both astonishingly beautiful and horrendously deadly, sometimes at the same time. If you want to progress with the control of the natural world around you, coming to terms with this fact is essential. You cannot master control of the creatures, or to some extent the elements around you, without this harsh truth. Never forget that though you may take hold of the world around you, it is still kill or be killed for many of these creatures. I've only shown you harmless creatures today, but can you imagine if you were employing the hive mind with a bunch of tigers, or snakes or hippos and you lost control for a split second? The consequences would be devastating, perhaps for you and perhaps for them. Learn well and this will not happen. Forget and you put yourself or your friends in danger."

I progressed quickly at this particular skill, I somehow could manage to really tune into Angela's different calls and replicate them with relative ease. I had bugs, birds and mice come to my call at the same rate as Grace and Robyn in no time, and it wasn't long after the first lesson that she'd decided that all three of us were ready for an underwater lesson.

She left the rest of the group in the hands of Grayson and marched us down to the seafront of the island. In a buried wooden box in the sand lay several wetsuits of different sizes, all looking a bit worn and dirty. I followed Grace's cautious lead and washed mine in the sea before putting it on, Robyn, oblivious, chatted to Angela as she put hers on without so much as a second glance at it. I saw a spider crawl over her neck. She either didn't notice or simply didn't care.

Once confident that we could all actually swim (all of us having some control over water helped enormously), Angela explained that the sea creature call is very different from air or land creatures, more of a low, baritone in your head that had to flow with the ocean itself to actually be heard by the fish. She demonstrated underwater, at first, we all looked perplexed at each other, nothing was heard inside, though fish did converge around her; eels, and other larger fish surrounded her, swimming playfully around her legs. We were still at a depth where you could just about stand on your tippy toes if you got tired, I was glad of it, as was Grace, Robyn was clearly the better swimmer out of us.

Angela explained that we would be able to tune in better in more dense waters. Gus was called via hive mind and had us speeding out into the open sea in no time, all of us crammed into his tiny wooden boat with no engine. After roughly a fifteen-minute ride out we each dropped from the tiny sail boat I had arrived on the island in and swam deeper under the waves.

Angela had been right, it was like turning up the volume. Out there, it was so much clearer what we had to do. Almost as if the sea was on a different radio frequency and the further out we got the less we had to tune out the land. We each took it in turns between swimming to the surface for breath; by the end of the day all three of us could call at least four or five fish to come to us, Robyn managed to get hers to do a dance around her head and made grace laugh, forgetting she was holding her breath, and had to be helped to the surface by Angela and Robyn as I laughed on the surface, it being my turn to rest and hold on to the boat. I earned a giant wave of water over my head from Grace.

We were chatty and positive on the way back, each feeling like we'd made a lot of progress, there was nothing we each couldn't do at least a little bit of now: air, fire, earth and water and having hive minds with every type of animal, land, air and sea. We felt powerful, like nothing could stop us. But the closer we got to the island, the more we tuned in. The more we realised something was off. A dank, stony feeling filled our stomachs. We stopped laughing abruptly and Gus sped the boat up with our help. No words were needed. We just needed to get back.

The island grew closer and closer, we could just about see the outline of Kit's cottage on the highest point. We were already at the point where we could tune into everybody else; fear. No individual conversations, no words, just raw emotion. We looked at Angela, who looked at Gus, he said inside his mind to stay on the boat. Then changed his mind and was louder when he said jump into the water and hold onto the boat. We did as he said. He wanted us to look like just some old guy minding his own business fishing. He got out his fishing gear and threw a line, his eyes focused on the cottage. There were tall grasses all round it, all we could make out were two figures near the edge. Gus narrowed his eyes, but didn't get any closer.

A crack like thunder was heard, then unmistakeably a male scream of anguish. Heart-breaking and hallowing to hear. Then we all saw it, a very small figure, falling as if in slow motion from the cliff's edge.

The Boy

Robyn gave a small scream as she scrabbled up to the boat, all of us following, not speaking as we shot the boat as fast as we could in the direction of the beach, it must have been the fastest that boat had ever gone, and it still wasn't fast enough. We all lost the signal of the small body on its impact to the rocks below. Its last minds thoughts blur of confusion, fright and the rushing sound of air. A terrible silence followed.

We got to the shore and the girls ran to the body, followed by Angela franticly trying to perform CPR. Myself and Gus stayed by the boat looking towards the cliff where the child had fallen. A man now stood there and looked over to the body on the rocks, he had a scarf covering half his face. There was no mistaking it; he was the one from the vision myself and the girls had. He stood with clenched fists, and was about to shout something behind himself, then locked eyes with me. I felt his stare like a powerful punch in the gut, I found myself actually moved back with the force of it, who was he? My gut was trying to tell me something.

He also looked as if he had the same feeling, his eyes confused and angry for a split second. He seemed to be making a quick decision in his head. He waved his arm around his head, encasing himself in what looked like the same glowing orbs from our visions, except that this time it was encasing his whole body, it flashed an unbelievable white, then he was gone.

***

The child's name was Andy. He had come to the island with his mother, a woman named Caroline. They both could control fire, nothing else. No way for the poor child to have saved himself from the fall. People talked and shared stories of the small family leading up to the funeral. The generally accepted truth was that they had both fled from an abusive father and husband. The boy's father had one drink too many one night and Caroline had to protect her son from being hit, and had found that she ignited the bottle that was thrown at them, and was able to do some damage to her husband before she and Andy ran for it. Andy, a timid boy, had no idea he had powers until he came to the island with his mother.

We took it in shifts to keep an eye on the grieving mother. She was often heard screaming in the night for her boy. She had to be moved to a metal cabin, brought in especially for her, as she had put so much fire damage to her own quarters and had started to endanger others with her subconscious agonising grief in sleep.

One night she was heard on the beach, a tyrant of flame and fire around her, she howled, "What good can come of this? Why, why, why, why, WHY. WHERE IS MY BOY?" The whole camp was woken and the best of the people with power over water stood on the edge of the cliff side, looking down on her with great sympathy as they washed her flames away, with a combined effort of soft rain and drawing great laps from the nearby sea. All she said for her burns was, "I couldn't save him, I deserve this.".

Caroline stayed with Kit for a while after that, Kit had the facilities in her lab to deal with most injuries we had on the island, including grade four burns. It was seen as the right place for Caroline to be, both mothers having lost their children. Kit comforted her with words of genomes and DNA, and how it couldn't possibly be her fault that she couldn't save him. But it was also overheard that Kit was trying to persuade Caroline to let her do some tests on the never before available dead body of someone with a gift. This made some people shout out with disgust. Caroline however, was persuaded, "If this helps just one person in the future, Andy's death will not be for nothing," she stammered through vacant eyes.

When the funeral came around, it was a calm and warm evening. Gus had dug the hole next to Kit's grandfather's grave, right at the far end of the island, where you could see the sun set. Caroline had wanted her boy there as she wanted him to have Kit's grandfather protect him. She didn't want him to be alone.

We all stood by the graves in as dark a clothing as we had available, as Kit spoke; "Here we are gathered, to mourn and remember our wonderful boy Andrew. He departed this world on unjust terms, I will do everything I can to ensure the safety of every last one of you, but alas, I was unable to that day. The pursuit of science is noble, no matter what the emotions of certain situations. We must find the answers. For us, for the children of the future and for Andrew."

"Many of you have asked what happened on that fateful day. I believe now is the right time to divulge that information, with the consent of Caroline, of course." Caroline, gave a watery nod with her now severely burnt face. "It is not my pleasure to inform you all of this, but we have an enemy out there. This person wants nothing more than to see every last one of us perish." The funeral silence stiffened somewhat at these words. "He is one of us, but a rouge, and highly dangerous. That day he came to the island specifically to wreak havoc and injure as many as he could, he found myself first and poor Andrew was simply playing in the trees nearby. Andrew had no idea of the danger he was in until it was too late. I naively thought that this man would not go so far as to hurt a child, I was wrong and will never, ever, forget it, or forgive myself for that matter."

"But that is merely one story of Andrew's life—" Kit went on to explain Andy's upbringing and most memorable moments. Myself, Grace and Robyn however instantly clicked in together with our separate hive mind.

"Something's not right," remarked Robyn.

"Definitely," I agreed, "What a load of horse shi—"

"Poop, Grace. Horse poop," corrected Robyn.

Kit's explanation definitely had holes, that much we all knew. Some random Guy just turns up out of the blue and wants to hurt everyone on the island, but finds her first, kills a young boy and then leaves. Why not stay on and continue the rampage, as dark as it sounded? Why go for Kit first when there were surely easier targets littered all over the place? Why now? We all agreed to meet up after the funeral, as chores and lessons were off for the day and discuss it further.

Visions

As soon as it was deemed polite to leave the mourning group by the main fire pit, we wandered off to our cabin, feeling morose. Out of us Robyn seemed the most affected by the events. She had a brother of around Andy's age back at home. Grace showed her feelings with anger and determination to find a solution to the threat of our new enemy. I was a mix of both, feeling both sadness and a disquiet in my head, I just could not shake the feeling that something was off about the whole situation. I was glad my two friends felt the same.

Back at the cabin a plan was formulated; first we ought to gather as much information about this Guy in the scarf from others on the island. There was bound to be extra snippets of information that others knew. Surely someone else must have seen what went on at the top of the cliffs. After that, we weren't quite sure. We had to find this murderer somehow, but what would happen when we did? Robyn suggested that he might just 'off' us too as soon as he saw us. Grace was adamant we could take him, 'Three unified girls against one puny man? Please, he doesn't stand a chance'. Grace and Robyn bickered for a moment dissecting our skill range and the likelihood of success. I stared out of the window, willing myself to think of some intelligent plot that was bound to work. Nothing came. My frustration mounted. Then just as I was turning away, I saw a light shining in the woods through the window. A double take confirmed; a glowing orb, graceful and radiant, shone through the murk of the night.

Grace and Robyn stopped arguing immediately, seeing my image in their heads and walked over to my window, intrigued. "Brilliant, off we go then!" exclaimed Grace with a huge grin.

"Not so fast, what if it's that guy, just tricking us?" Robyn said, always the cautious one.

"Do you honestly think that this is a trick, do you think we're about to get killed?" I asked.

"No."

"Well, stop fannying about then, and let's go already!" Grace enthused.

We shoved our jackets and shoes on and followed the light, which was now almost out of sight, we did a lazy girl, half-jog until we caught up with it.

It was leading us to the spot where we had all first had a joint vision. We all guessed what was to come. The orb, about waist height, moved to the middle of our clearing and we all stood around it, waiting. I knew we'd done the right thing as soon as I felt myself involuntarily lift upwards. Grace and Robyn followed, I had that shaky, but warm feeling through my whole body like slipping from wakefulness to a dream, we were in a trance state once more.

Light filled the area around us now, all things surrounded by misty, bright fog. We were in that peculiar but wonderful place again, I tried to figure out how long it had taken, but time did strange things there. The glowing fire raged in the middle of us, blue-white in colour and silent. As mesmerising as before. Each of us stared into the flames. The images came thick and fast this time, almost too many to remember. First, we saw things we had each already seen; the picture in Kit's lab of her and her deceased son, images of the island itself as seen from the beach inland and Kit going down into her lab with Caroline. The visions got faster and faster after that as if the fire had a lot to tell us in very little time, the sense of urgency grew as each of the images was shown to us; a young man arguing with Kit and leaving the island on a boat. My buck, leading me to my first trance, where I discovered I had powers and got my marks on my arm, though the fire showed me a close up of the fire there and then went underground where the fire had been and showed a glowing stone with markings on it. Grace's was next with her horse, leading her to the banks of a great lake, under her fire too was a stone with different markings. Robyn was last with her fox leading her to a fire being on the top of either a large hill or small mountain, her stone lay in the same place as Grace's and mine. Then an image came of all of us with the stones in hand, triumphant. Then images of the man in the scarf on a vessel, like a small sailing boat. Other images of Kit on the phone fuming with rage. An army helicopter, the kind with two propellers, landing on the island. And finally, an image of myself, alone and terrified looking, covered in dirt and blood. We all fell to the floor this time in utter exhaustion, panting heavily. This time we felt drained and scared. A very contrasting experience compared to when we all unified for the first time.

"I can't believe it, it can't be, she said he was dead!" Robyn shook her head in disbelief. It was clear from the things we had just been shown, the boy in the picture, the boy arguing with her, the man on the boat, clearly older, was Kit's son. The same man who killed Andy. "Why wouldn't she just tell us at the funeral? I don't get it."

"Because Robyn, she needs us to trust her, if we don't put our faith in her this whole place goes to pieces, imagine how it would sound to Caroline, or anyone else for that matter, to find out the woman who's been comforting her has a secret son who just killed her child?" I retorted.

"Exactly, everyone would run away and spread stories of this place, we'd all be found out and then who knows?" agreed Grace.

"The real question is why did he run away from her in the first place, no kid leaves their own mother at that age without serious good reason." I continued.

"Is it that Kit's mental or is it that he's evil?" Grace pondered, almost to herself.

"What about the stones? We saw a stone before in our first trance, remember? Do you think they're really there, under our first trance sites?" Robyn asked.

"Only one way to find out." I eyed them both.

"I say screw digging around about this guy for a few days, we need to go tonight. I didn't like the look of that army chopper coming, we don't have time to waste here." Grace spoke with extreme confidence, I nodded enthusiastically and Robyn dolefully agreed too.

It was clear our first prerogative was to find each of our stones, after that we would set out to find Kit's son, at least we had some sort of clue as to where he was now, he definitely resided on a boat a lot of the time. We agreed that we wouldn't have been shown him there for no reason, it had to be a hint. We now also had reason to believe what his motives could be, a definite falling out with his mother, that's why he went for her first, we decided.

We each set about frantically gathering all the possessions we would need, leaving behind a great deal at the same time. We weren't sure how long we'd need to be gone so a raid of the food store was made also. On our door Robyn insisted that we leave a note explaining our absence and the missing food and our apologies and that we would be back soon, we just needed a break from the island after what happened, yadda, yadda, ya. No need to tell her what we were really up to, we still didn't know what to make of the visions we had of Kit.

We crept down to the shore, Gus's boat was in its usual place on the dock he himself had built. "Sorry Gus." Grace whispered as she untied the ropes and unceremoniously chucked her bags in. Myself and Robyn climbed in and together we unified our powers to drive the boat forward. We sped off into the cold night, away from Living Stone Island.

Finding the Stones

Once on the shore, we walked to the communal village car park where Robyn spotted what we needed; a typical old lady car, bound to be full to the brim of fuel and easy to break into, an old-looking green Micra, no cameras in sight. Grace had brought all she needed to hot wire a car and she set to work as myself and Robyn kept a lookout, not that there was anyone about at four in the morning in a sleepy coastal village.

After about half an hour Grace was in and we heard the engine give a shaky start. Robyn left a note with her address under a rock where the car had been parked, we planned to do a sort of treasure hunt so the poor old biddy that owned it would eventually get it back, when we were done with it. With myself and Robyn racked with guilt and Grace finally looking excited we drove into the mountains to find Robyn's first trance location, as hers was the closest.

It was just beginning to show signs of daybreak when we arrived in a small market town. A pretty high street with Victorian looking roof tops and non-chain supermarkets lay amongst the hills. We turned down towards the end of the street into a small row of houses, Grace was driving and sensed that Robyn wanted her to slow up. A light was on in one of the houses with the blinds open. Inside could be seen a large dining table with five plates set, a woman, man and two younger boys all sat having an incredibly early breakfast. Grace stopped the car on the opposite side of the street. I clocked the missing person. She was in the car with us, a face brimming with tears. "We rise early to deal with the sheep," Robyn choked. I knew her family to be farmers.

"Why don't you pop in and say hi, for heaven's sake?" retorted Grace, frustrated at our friend's sorrow.

"Not everyone has a bad family Grace," she suddenly snapped. "If I went in there and just showed my face after two years of nothing, they'd want to know everything, it would terrify them. They'd be scared of me. I can't do that to them, or myself."

"But you have an opportunity right now, just take it, jeez."

"Grace just because you don't understand doesn't mean I'm wrong okay?" Robyn sneered at Grace, it was the first time I'd ever seen her this angry. They had little tiffs all the time, but this was real anger.

"Are you saying I'm thick? Great, now I know how you really feel. Why don't we just drop the pretence all together?"

"Grace, if I went in there right now, I'd put them all at risk and you know it, you're only saying this because you feel sorry for yourself, it's not my fault you have a rubbish family, can't you just let me have this moment, without ruining it for me?" Grace remained silent for a moment. I looked between both of them.

"She's right, Grace, we have no idea what we're chasing right now, if this guy finds out there are people he can use against us, we're screwed."

"Yeah, well maybe it'd be nice to have someone he could use against me. I've got no one. Never have done, probably never will," Grace lamented.

"You've got us, pissy pants. You idiot." Robyn snorted; half angry, half amused, "brainy bum."

"Grumble grinch."

"Guys, they're looking!" I saw what must have been Robyn's youngest brother pointing out the window at our car, our lights stupidly still on in the dark morning. We drove at break neck speed away from Robyn's family.

Having made up in their own unique way the journey continued for a few miles, until Robyn told us to pull over in a very bumpy layby at the foot of what she had called a 'medium sized hill'. It looked much more like a mountain to me and Grace. Like a *Country File* presenter, Robyn stepped out of the car, took a deep nasally breath, hands on hips and said enthusiastically, "Come on then!" Grace and I, about a metre or so behind her, trudged on.

The 'medium-sized hill' was at least not as difficult as I thought, there were lots of tussocks and rocks to scramble onto and get your footing and the climb was made much easier by the ever-increasing light. It finally broke into sunrise as we reached the very top. It was hard not to feel moved by nature's spectacle. The dew on the grass shone like diamonds and the sounds of birds filled the air as they too woke from the cold night.

Robyn walked around for a few minutes trying to recall where exactly the fire had been in her vision two years ago. Grace was getting impatient and was worried that in the daylight some one might think it odd that an unlocked Micra was in a random country layby, one of the only passing places for a good, few yards. "Finished soul searching yet?" she called out.

"It was ages ago, give me a break! Feel free to start digging by all means, I haven't got a clue where it was, all traces of a fire have long gone by now!" Robyn grabbed her red hair in frustration and started walking in tight circles, with a slightly mad look in her eye.

I grabbed Grace's hand and lead her forward to where Robyn stood, and grabbed hers too. They gave me a look of instant understanding. This must be a good way to find it. We closed our eyes and unified our minds, searching through Robyn's memories. As we travelled backwards in her own personal time line, we saw flashes of mealtimes at the island, where she was happiest, cooking for everyone, seeing their smiles. We saw images of all three of us practising our powers and laughing, an image of Grace slipping over in the mud of winter, eventually we got to her journey to the island and an image showed of her looking at her sleeping family, presumably for the last time. I felt Grace's guilt shine through at that point. On and on it went until we pinpointed Robyn coming up to the mountain with her fox, shivering in only a t-shirt in the night, she looked younger but her face of constant optimism was still there. Then we saw the fire, it was in between three very distinctive looking rocks with flattish tops. Grace tore away from the hive mind and shouted, "Over there!" We had only been a few feet away from them this whole time.

Relieved, Robyn unpacked the foldaway shovel from her bag, (a useful find of mine before we left, one of the kids on the island loved metal detecting), she dug into the soil and found it was incredibly stony and hit only rock. We knew it would have to be done with powers but were all apprehensive of accidentally breaking the one particular stone we were looking for. They looked at me as I had shown the best control over earth in our classes. I felt the pressure, but was confident in my work. I stilled my mind and instead of focusing on breaking the rocks, concentrated on retrieving Robyn's stone, picturing the vision we had in my mind of what it looked like, or thereabouts. I heard a crack, like a truck on snow, the ground had opened up. Through the chasm I had made rose a glowing pebble, the size of a small egg with a symbol on it, it looked to be a triangle with a line across the top. Robyn stood over myself and Grace, as we knelt on the ground and held her hand under the levitating stone. She let it plop into her outstretched hand.

All Together

Grace didn't want to waste any time away from the precious Micra, so as soon as we had the stone, we left. After a small debate on the ethics of either hot wiring another car or carrying on with the Micra it was decided that we should leave a note at Robin's house directing whoever owned it to the next house we were going to; mine. We kidded ourselves that it would be fun for whoever's car we had stolen.

I was more than a little apprehensive to be heading 'home'. Me and my mother had never exactly gotten on, I found myself wondering if she missed me at all, or if it was just a convenient story to tell her friends. She fed on drama like a leech. Or perhaps I was just painting her in the worst light possible because I couldn't stand the thought of her caring for me after a childhood of seemingly obnoxious disinterest, it would make this as hard as it was for Robyn. At that moment, it was easier to feel abandoned like Grace, nothing lost.

Robyn took her turn driving, she was a lot more road conscious than Grace and the journey was somewhat slower and more frustrating with Grace huffily muttering under her breath about Robyn's driving etiquette. "I don't know about you, but I want to draw the least amount of attention to this car as possible, the faster we go and the more laws we break the better the chance we could get caught, so shut it."

"You're just as likely to draw attention to this car by going forty on a national speed limit road, numb nuts." I silenced the bickering between them by announcing the turning for my village. I suggested we park down an old farmer's track that I knew people rarely went down, it seemed safer in broad daylight than a layby, at least the car was hidden that way.

The day was getting to be warmer as I lead them through the buck's passage in the hedge and along the river that lined the forest. As my trance was the most recent it really wasn't a challenge for me to find my fire spot. Twenty minutes after we had set out, all three of us were looking at the small remnants of my woodland fire that had happened not even six months ago. I didn't even need to use the shovel, I simply dug my hand into the slightly ashy mud, which was soft from the river nearby. After some awkward squelchy sounds, I felt a smooth, surprisingly warm stone in my hand against the chilled soil. With glee I pulled it out and rushed over to the river to wash off the dirt. My symbol was similar to Robyn's, only it was a reverse of hers; an upside down triangle, with a line near the bottom. We took a moment to wonder what they both meant. Grace suggested it meant we were both holding her up and we got a move on once more. Grace didn't like to be last in anything or left out in anyway, I suspected this was torture for her.

We did the same as before for our poor owner of the car and left a note with Grace's address in the letter box of my house before we drove off once more. As it was my turn to drive I insisted that we take some of the spare petrol from my mother's mower from the garden shed, she appeared to be out so we were safe-ish in doing this. The combination for the lock was the same, although it wouldn't have been hard to bust our way through, powers or not. Feeling quite successful we rewarded ourselves with a much-needed food break after an hour's driving, having not been so much as suspiciously looked at yet we felt like nothing could go wrong in our pursuit. We inwardly thanked

Angie for making such good bread, and Gus for always taking the time to fetch things like crisps and chocolate bars from the mainland.

Much of the journey had to be done on B-roads as going through major towns and cities was a no-no for us, so the journey to Grace's house took the longest. By the time we had reached it the day was nearly over. For some reason we all felt it important that we find all the stones on the same day.

Grace's house was nestled in the largest town so far, down some rough looking back streets with wheelie bins coating the front of the houses instead of pretty little gardens. Her face was that of distain as I drove past her old abode. I slowed and pulled up to a few cars opposite her house and waited for her to say something. Grace looked shaken as she stared at the house. "They've moved." She spoke in almost a whisper. Robyn and I saw a young couple pulling up to the drive and doing the whole, 'we can carry all the shopping in, in one go' manoeuvre. Her mother and step dad had moved house knowing she was missing. The lack of concern they must have had shocked even me. I felt suddenly very guilty of feeling somewhat sorry for myself about my own mother. Robyn didn't know what to say. What could you say? "Let's just go." Grace said defiantly, determined to be strong. "We could ask them if they know where your mum moved to?" I said, cringing at my own feeble attempt to rectify Grace's mood. "Drive." Was her reply. So, I did.

Grace numbly directed me to the lake, a twenty-minute excursion from the town's cul-de-sac estates. She grew more hopeful as we got closer and soon her mind was all consumed by the hunt for the last stone, her stone. She reminisced for a while, telling us of the horse that had found her right outside her house after the incident with her stepdad. How it had led her to this spot and how, like us it had felt more like a dream than reality. We reached the narrower roads and pulled up near a bridal way that led us down a steep slope, the sun was behind the surrounding hills now and the lake before us, at the very bottom of the bowl we stood in, was still and dark. After a jaunty clamber down Grace had no difficulty in finding her spot where her fire had been; directly in the middle, in the lowest part of the sloping fields was a small dip in the ground where the grass was shorter. Robyn extracted the foldaway shovel and Grace's stone was found about a foot under the soil.

Grace's stone, was again, like mine and Robyn's; small and egg shaped with a symbol on it, a triangle with one side larger than the other two, hers had no line through it. As she held it she exclaimed with glee that she felt it warm to the touch. We had all tried to feel the warmth of mine and Robyn's stone before and felt nothing, it appeared that only the person who it was meant for could feel its heat.

Just before the sun had completely set, we all held our stones outstretched in front of us. Myself and Robyn had not held ours much in front of Grace knowing her tension in finding hers last. This was the first time we had seen all of them together. A warm breeze surrounded us, whipping our hair and clothes, though the grasses and other foliage around us remained still. All three of us standing together, it was clear that the next step was to slip back into our own hive mind. We were all feeling a little more apprehensive this time though, it felt very different now with the stones, we were certain that it wouldn't be the usual trance.

Grace was the first to take a tentative step closer to us, she held my marked arm, holding her stone with the other in the middle of our small circle. I followed, grabbing Robyn's marked arm and holding out my stone in the other hand. Robyn paused for a fraction, swallowed, and finally did the same, uniting us. The warm breeze grew faster and became a violent torrent of wind around us, we had to steady ourselves for fear of being blown over. I felt Robyn's mark suddenly become as hot like the worst sunburn you've ever had. I could tell the other's felt this too, the last thing I saw in the real world was Grace mouthing, "Don't let go!" The wind was so strong around us now that I couldn't hear her voice. Water from the lake nearby was sucked into our mini vortex and pebbles and tufts of grass from the ground were picked up, causing a hurricane effect, just as I thought it was all too much the stone shone as bright as a chemical reaction, blinding us. The force of the whirlwind around us got so strong I felt my hand rip away from Robyn's and Grace's hand left my arm. My stone seemed superglued in my other hand as it forcefully flew me backwards. Expecting to land hard on the grounds by the lake I braced myself for the impact. But none came.

Spirit World

Extremely disorientated, I felt my ears adjust to a new altitude. My hair brushed my face as if underwater and I instinctively held my breath. As I opened my eyes though I found I was not submerged in water, or really in complete air. The atmosphere was definitely somewhere in between. I looked down at my clothes and they rippled gently in the faintly foggy climate. I expected to be standing on clouds, this was surely heaven or somewhere similar, and we had all made a huge mistake and simultaneously died when we had united the stones, but the ground was there, also covered in this strange, thick air.

I looked around, popped my stone into my trouser pocket, and saw great trees with gnarled bark, wider and taller than most houses. I had landed near a root of one said tree and its circling nature was something I had never seen before at home. The trees appeared to move gently, as if breathing, their branches and roots ever so slowly moving around the colossal rocks they had grown around and into. 'Earth' I thought, as I reached out to the tree that had cradled my fall into this new, unfamiliar land. Like a stop motion picture, I saw a new bud grow from its trunk and gently touched it as it grew before me, it coiled around my marked arm, as if saying hello. As I dropped my arm the growth moved with me, then slowed as I moved away. In this place everything was one.

I needed to find Grace and Robyn, it seemed to make sense that they would be closer to a source of water, or high up in the air, as I was surrounded by my element, surely they would be too.

I wondered at the memory of the symbols on our stones, it had to have something to do with elements. As I turned, I saw huge swathes of vines clinging from the giant trees, flowers I'd never seen born of all colours I could have ever imagined, they bloomed and closed as I walked beneath them. My sheer presence affecting the flora around me. Sweet and unusual scents reached my nose from the plants, I found myself feeling heady and relaxed, nothing seemed threatening or worrisome. As I walked further through the land the ground became wetter and the air darker and thicker with foliage, just as I was finding it hard to see I reached out my hand and before my eyes grew large bioluminescent mushrooms, the most gorgeous sight. They creaked with their speed of growth, elated I span around using both my hands to grow more and more of these magnificent fungi until I was bathed in their soft glow.

Reaching the edge of a murky swamp, I easily made roots from trees within reach grow fatter for my ease of walking across them and was soon running along, changing my environment to suit my journey with such speed and agility I felt my power surge inside. I had no idea I could be this influential on the world around me. I sought to climb higher in the trees to better find my friends and see the extent of the new world we had landed in, when I heard an echoey male voice behind me, "Enjoying yourself?"

The vines I had created became lethally spiked in an instant of hearing the voice, like hairs on a cat's back, and all had pointed in the direction where he was; lying casually in a circular hollow of a tree not six foot away from me, eating some sort of foreign fruit. He was unmistakeably the man from Kit's photograph, the same one that had come to the island, killing that poor boy. Still wearing that stupid scarf over half his face.

I felt my features contract into a venomous rage. I threw my arms forward shooting the now thorned vines straight into his torso. He casually flicked his hand, the other still holding the fruit, and a wall of flame burned my vines into ashes in seconds. I was unharmed but twice as angry. "Look, you have to trust me right now, your actual bodies are in danger, listen to me and I can help you three."

"You killed Andy, why would I ever listen to you?" I broke a large hunk of rock off of a nearby ledge and hurled it at him, this time he actually had to dodge it and looked a little more intimidated, surprised at my violence, dropping the fruit.

"Look you don't understand, I'm not the bad guy here, if you would just listen—" I threw more chunks of rock at him, he appeared to make some sort of impenetrable bubble around himself with my rocks bending around an invisible force, I realised he must have more than one element under his sleeve. It was always best not to underestimate an enemy. I panted, waiting for his move, if he was ever going to make one.

"I don't have time to tell you everything right now, but please believe me when I say that Kit isn't what she seems, she founded Living Stone Island to use people like us for her benefit. Right now, your actual bodies back in the real world are in a lot of danger. You've left a bloody breadcrumb trail so it's only a matter of hours until Kit finds your bodies where you left them—"

"Where we left them? What are you on about, I'm right here!" I forgot to be afraid of him for a moment, and felt instead like laughing. His dark eyebrows knotted in frustration and he pulled his scarf down to reiterate his point.

"Kit's my mother, she did this to me when I wouldn't do the programme. I was seven years old." My features softened in shock when I saw a grotesque scar going from the right side of his face, just below his nostril to his neck, it hadn't been stitched and had healed badly, leaving an almost inch wide jagged line down his face. Lies were easier to spot with the hive mind, he let me search. He was telling the truth. I saw Kit making her child back away into the corner of her lab in fear as she shouted, tears ran down his face as he cowered away from her, I had to stop just as Kit lunged for him. It was heart breaking to see, I wouldn't watch the rest.

My thorns retreated. I didn't think his scarf was stupid any more.

"Hi, I'm Mark." He said to diffuse the unease. He covered his face once more.

"Hi, I'm Millie." I replied. Then added, because curiosity was killing me, "Where are we?"

"We're currently in the spirit world. It lies in a parallel plain to our universe. Here your soul is present, but not your body. As I can see you've noticed you have accelerated power here. I'm still not sure why we can access it, but I'm working on it." He suddenly strongly reminded me of Kit's own impertinence with her own research. I reasoned he must have her intelligence.

"Right, so where is my body?" I looked at my hands, confused, they were very much there in front of me.

"In the field by the lake you all transferred in. So far, I've devised that the stones are the only thing that can actually 'hop' worlds. What you have in your pocket is the real deal, they don't stay with your physical body."

"You have one too?" He held out his stone, its marking was a triangle, right side up, the opposite to Graces. He dropped his protective air orb around him as I came closer, trusting me this time. "What do the markings men?" I was keen to get all the answers I could.

"You really haven't figured that out?" His eyes smiled. Slowly, like talking to a four-year-old, he pointed to his stone and said, "F-I-R-E", then to mine, and said, "Eaaarrrrrth."

"Very funny. Grace's is water and Robyn's is air, right?"

"Correct. The triangles are all ancient symbols used for the elements."

"So what do the trances mean? Why us, why now?"

"Easy, I told you we don't have time, we have to get your body back before Kit finds you."

"No."

"What?"

"No, we've got to get the stones first, she'll want those more than she wants us, I'm sure of it."

"But your friends—"

"They'll understand, and they can handle themselves. Besides if we're quick enough we can save them and the stones, come on."

I grew the branch we stood on, some thirty feet above the ground and took us both high above the canopy of trees. Once there we could see the vastness of the jungle around us, as I suspected a dark shape of Grace was seen by a large body of water — a wide, rumbling river. She had evidently found Robyn already and was showing off her skills with water. I heard Robyn laugh as Grace dropped her water orb she was making, drenching them both. Grace had seen us high above the trees. It was Mark's turn to look surprised, "You guys really aren't grasping the seriousness of the situation."

"Oh, come off it she's just having a little fun."

Mark grabbed me and made a circle of air around us, only visible by the small bits of bracken and leaves kept up in the draft around us. We glided down to where Robyn and Grace stood, I connected with them before we hit the ground sharing my most recent memoires with them to save both time and Mark from further attacks. As soon as we reached them Robyn went into overdrive panic, "But this means we can't possibly go back to the island! What about the others? What are we going to do? We have to help them!" Robyn was already showing signs of near hyperventilation, holding her heart looking at everyone frantically. The air around her whirled in panic and we all got faces full of forest as she soared into a frenzy of dread.

Grace grabbed her by the arms and shook her, "Robyn I can't think with you doing that!"

They started to argue, as time was of the essence, I separated them and screamed, "QUIET." They both stopped mid-sentence immediately with comical half insults ready to come out of their mouths. "We need to get back to our bodies, right? But we also need to make sure Kit doesn't get hold of the stones."

"You only need one to get back into the spirit world, I'd say your safest bet was to hide two of them here, and only keep one." Mark reasoned. We looked at each other, and smiled as we all co-thought at the same time; 'Rock, paper scissors'. After an intense battle, I was reigning champion and so kept mine while Robyn and Grace reluctantly hid theirs within a small hollow underneath a nearby bush that had some of the strange fruit Mark had been eating on it. "Okay, so my body is currently hidden a few yards from you three by the lake in the real world—"

"You were following us?!" Grace was outraged.

"Well, you didn't exactly make it hard." Mark raised his eyebrow.

"Why don't we all just get back there, come on people, let's go, go, go!" Robyn was beyond panicked now. Mark held his stone, and in a flash, disappeared. We held arms as before and were surprised to find the transit much quicker and much more straight forward in the spirit world. The world rushed around us, and in a moment, we were gone.

Collecting the Bodies

I awoke feeling much more tired and bruised than I had done in the spirit world, and very hot. Flame surrounded my body. I jumped up, stricken at the sudden change in atmosphere, something wasn't right, were we too late? I looked for my friends and Mark, beyond the wall of flame that surrounded me I could just about make out Mark and Kit having an extraordinary fight, Mark using fire and air to battle Kit's masterful use of earth and water. A large army helicopter with its powerful engine still on had landed in the field, the wind of its blades only fuelling the fire around me. It took all my strength and willpower to summon some of the water from the lake to douse my prison of flame, I realised I hadn't eaten since lunch and was too weak not to use my strongest element, how much easier things had been in the spirit world. I had a brainwave and remembered Grace mocking me about having to use tunnels to beat the traffic and get to work on time. I inwardly thanked her as I used my power over the earth to forge an escape route.

Once out I saw several men in dark clothing and body armour trying to capture Grace and Robyn, I was sent into a red heat of power and anger, not caring if I maimed or killed in trying to help them. One of the men had Robyn by the neck and instead of helping herself at a crucial moment she chose to use a blast of air to knock back another attacker from behind me and screamed "RUN." whilst flailing her legs, out of energy, to fight back. I refused to back down, and solidified the man holding her, with grasses, knotting around his legs, I brought him down to the ground where the long strands encased his neck and arms. We ran to Grace who was fighting off two at once, using powerful jets from the lake to almost drown her attackers where they stood; choking and gasping for air one of them used Grace's power to his advantage before we could reach her. Using his taser he managed to electrocute himself and Grace by holding it to the jet of water she was controlling over his face, Grace curled in pain and her face was motionless as she fell hard on to the ground, her body convulsing. Robyn went in to hold her, tears falling, not noticing the men behind her, I thwacked them with the lake-side rocks, managing to knock two of them out, the one that remained had a gun and was aiming at me when Robyn outright punched him in the gut, winding him but was shot in the back by another, I stood terrified and saw a feathery dart in her back, a tranquilliser. Suddenly we were surrounded by over twenty of these men, we were cornered in every possible way. The men grabbed my friends' bodies away from me and simply pushed me to the ground when I tried to fight them, exhausted.

I heard a harrowing scream from Kit and an alarm sounded, the men's priorities had shifted to her, I looked in the direction they ran; Kit was like a witch burning on a stake. A whistle above me was all I needed to know it was Mark, with the last of my reserves I made the air around me give me a boost to his arm, he grabbed me mid-air in his orb, and I last saw Grace and Robyn being loaded onto the helicopter while the men tried to put out the flame around Kit. We disappeared from the scene with no one watching, alone together. Both having failed.

***

We ran to the roadside and behind a barn where Mark had hidden a motor bike, he handed me his helmet and said briskly, "Get on." I cried the whole journey, not registering where we were going. Feeling the most alone I had felt in months. I had failed my only friends, the people who would have done anything for me. How had we been so stupid? I felt immense guilt for mucking around in the spirit world, letting my ego get the best of me, making giant luminescent mushrooms instead of rushing to help my friends for crying out loud. I felt the shame like a slime, coating my whole body. I tried to reach them with our hive mind, whether it was because we were too far apart now, or because they were both unconscious, I wasn't sure, but I couldn't get through to them.

I wasn't sure how much time had passed since we got on the bike, I started to feel the call of the sea and figured if we were by the ocean it must have been hours. Mark abandoned the bike in a hedge and told me to follow. I couldn't tell if he was more frustrated at me or himself. I welcomed his rage, I deserved it. "It wasn't your fault, I'm not angry at you." I'd forgotten he could do that.

"Well perhaps you should be."

"I somehow don't think you can blame yourself for not being able to fight off that many experienced squaddies Millie, we were outnumbered, I wasn't even expecting that kind of show from her, she's hard enough to fight on her own, let alone with an army to back her up. We'll get them back, I promise."

I came back to my senses and realised we had been walking to the end of a harbour. I saw the almost rotting wooden decking I was standing on, covered in lichen and moss. There was nowhere to go but the ocean from here. I looked quizzically at

Mark, he just smiled and paused by a boat. I looked at it, large enough to live in, but not massive, "Mark I've really had enough of stealing things today, can we not?"

"Who said anything about stealing? She's all mine." Of course, it was the boat from the vision.

The Truth About Kit

As Mark untied the ropes holding the boat to the harbour with methodical ease, I wondered how on earth he could afford such an object. Kit spoke as if she came from an upper class, and clearly had money judging from her extensive laboratory, I assumed Mark must have had some sort of trust fund.

He hauled in his large bag first and then leapt on board himself, ushering me to do the same. "Where exactly are we going?" I asked, exhausted and numb after the night's events.

"Far. But from what I hear she can't track us with you anyway, so we should be pretty safe even if we chose to stay one or two miles from the shore." He spoke as if I was in on whatever he was getting at. I recalled a dim memory of Kit saying I was hard to track on my travels to the island. I persevered through my fatigue, my curiosity conquering my lack of sleep.

"If she can't track me then how did she find us at the lake? How does she 'track' people anyway? Do we all have chips in us?" My horror was noticeable.

"Ha, you've got a very vivid imagination, the truth is much more interesting though." He spoke happily as he untied various complicated knots on the deck, getting us ready for departure. "My mother's always been able to sniff out people like us, she knew I was one instantly and she can feel it when another is born sometimes, or other times it's when they first use their powers, tends to vary on the potency of the gift that particular person has. She was conducting research on a shark's ability to do the same when I left. Sharks can detect the electrical charge of animals that they're very far away from, for hunting purposes. She was pretty certain her ability to find everyone with powers was linked in some way to a shark's own abilities."

"So she literally hunts us down?"

"Yeah, but she couldn't ever get a clear signal on you. You were lucky you left the island when you did, when I arrived, she was in her lab mucking around with your DNA. I think it was only a matter of time before she could have wanted to do some of her unique brand of tests on you. But with science you always need a control group, that's where that poor kid came in to play, so to speak. She used the hive mind to call me to her, knowing I would always come if someone was in danger. She did it because she needed someone to blame for his death." Mark stopped tying his knots at this point and looked out to the sea, clearly upset.

The truth drenched me like a wave, "She killed him. She killed him on purpose, didn't she?" Mark, unable to put it into words, simply showed me his memory of that day.

He and Kit were having a whispered row in her lab, Mark pleading with Kit to not go ahead with some deal she had made. Kit angrily retorted with arguments about science being more important than petty feelings, and answers that were needed had to come from sacrifice. She had Caroline's little boy in the lab with them, looking positively terrified. Mark screamed that she was insane and freed the boy from the lab table, and climbed the ladder to outside. Mark stood between the boy and Kit on the edge of the cliff, ready to take the boy to safety, Kit let out an unholy screech and broke the rock away from where the boy had stood, letting him fall rather than having everyone know the truth. Mark conjured his air orb and was gone in a flash.

We both stood in the chilly air silent. "You have no idea how strong she is. She rarely uses her power in front of others for a reason. You saw at the lake, I could barely fight her then. Every time I've tried, I've failed, leaving someone either dead or captured." Mark spat through gritted teeth.

"Mark, it's not your faul—"

"If I had been quicker, I could have saved him, it's a fact. I just have to learn to live with it. You can get some sleep down in the bunk, I'll stay up here for a bit." I knew this was guy talk for 'I need some space', so I did as I was told, as we slowly sailed away, grateful for the opportunity to sleep. My thoughts dragged me back to that day, Andy falling, but the heavy waves of sleep won in the end.

***

I woke with a warm midday sun on my face from one of the portholes in the boat's side. I must have had a good eight or nine hours. It took me a while to realise why I was so conflicted and upset. Then the previous day's memories crept back like an unwelcome rash.

I looked about my surroundings, I was lying in a single bed, with perhaps only two feet above me for head space, typical boat quarters. Every ounce of space was used for something, either tiny cupboards, work areas with stacks of papers, or used to hang towels. The walls were wooden slatted, but I could only see a fraction of this as the rest were covered in newspaper cuttings, diagrams and lists of information. Upon closer inspection I could see this was Mark's research wall, eerily similar to his mother's lab walls, only this was clearly in pursuit of finding out what she was up to, not finding all the other people with gifts.

I was looking through some pinned papers on the different projects he suspected her of undergoing, just catching an army logo on one of them, when I heard him clear his throat in the doorway. I was half inclined to congratulate him on his element of surprise to ease the tension, but he did so himself by handing me a steaming plate of eggs and bacon. Ravished, I consumed the lot within minutes and asked for seconds, as he too looked upon his wall of investigations. He ladled me down more eggs and bacon with a slightly overcooked sausage as well. "Have you not slept yet?" I asked.

"Hammock in the back room, it's comfy enough. I see you're interested in my research." He commented, not letting me get away with my snooping. I chewed extra slow, childishly avoiding the conversation. "It's okay, you're bound to have been curious, if I wanted it to be kept secret from you I wouldn't have taken the hammock, don't worry."

I swallowed, "Great because I have some questions." I stood, taking my breakfast with me and found the piece of paper with army credentials on it and a lot of very expensive bills with Kit's name next to them.

"Ah, I see you've found the worst and most incriminating piece of evidence first, you're good at this."

"What does it mean? What has your mother got to do with the army?"

"The question now, judging from the helicopter assistance yesterday, is what hasn't she got to do with the army." His brows creased in vexation. "By now you must have some sort of idea of the lengths my mother will go to, to get her answers. To conduct her science, if you will." I nodded. "Well, it appears she's had the bright idea of getting funding from the military. As far as I've been able to deduce, their deal is that they give her all the money and equipment she needs, and in return she shares her data with them. The end result eventually being an amalgamation of highly advanced super soldiers and the best kind of tracking tech they could ever wish for. Not to mention being able to possibly take enemy planes out of the sky with the power of air. Sink rival submarines with control over water, obliterate entire cities with earth and fire. With Kit's research, the military can and will have the power to destroy any enemy without the use of nukes, or the expense for that matter."

"Everyone on the island, they'll be, they'll be—"

"Probably being used as the first test batch super soldiers. The women have the worst to fear right now as the army will almost certainly be wanting more people with powers, this is evidence— 'He held up another piece of paper with a lot of chromosome information on it, '—that Kit has figured out how the specific genes are passed on, your friends may be used as hosts to grow more soldiers, as the genes are passed down through the mother's side."

All the information was too much to take in, somehow through the terror and confusion, my own mother's face popped into my mind. "My Mum! Oh my god, I never knew. Oh, Christ, I bet they've taken her!" I dropped my plate and felt exceedingly dizzy at this point. Mark pushed me down onto the single bed purely so I didn't collapse onto the floor.

He put his hand on my shoulder kneeling down and said, "Millie, this is the one area where we have the advantage, I'm not so bad at the whole science game either, when I was following you there I stopped by your mum's and observed her for a while, I couldn't connect with her mind at all. She isn't one of us. I think that's why you can't be tracked. You're unique in that, so far, you're the only one with powers that hasn't had them passed down through your family."

"Great I feel so darn special."

"Well, try to think of it as a huge advantage to defeating my mother, at the very least. The unique wavelength you emit seems to affect those around you as well, as we haven't been found yet." Mark spoke as if I was an ungrateful child. "Now stop sulking so we can actually figure out what on earth we're going to do about all this." He cleared the small work space with a brisk wave of his arm, papers flying to the floor, and handed me a pen. It seemed so useless, making a plan to catch what essentially was an evil scientist, and our high-tech planning equipment involved biro pens and scraps of paper to write on, on a tiny boat.

The Balance

The days grew steadily hotter as we worked. Our usual routine tended to be an awful lot of pacing on the small decks of Mark's boat in the early morning hours after a short stint of four or five hours of sleep, always invaded by stressful dreams. I would often hear Mark moan and grunt in his hammock, a few metres away from what had become my bedroom, and what was also the office where we calculated our plans. We had to be careful as any mistake could cost the lives of innocent people. The pressure was unreal.

Mark would become restless and frustrated with our lack of progress sometimes and take the small dingy to the mainland to fetch supplies of food and fresh drinking water. I was glad of the break usually, I always had to figure out my life on my own, thinking up a valid rescue mission was less intense without Mark looming over my shoulder continually asking what I thought of just winging it and arriving with no course of action figured out. A number of times I was sorely tempted to remind him of just how badly things went the last time he turned up on the island with no identifiable strategy.

After roughly a month of researching Kit's military influences, the names and identities of the people now premeditatedly on the island, holding my friends, captive, it seemed implausible that just two people could ever defeat her system in place. On a particularly muggy and damp day Mark strode up to me, I was sitting on the roof of the boat, twiddling my stone between my fingers, staring out to sea, he handed me some papers, still warm from the printer. I looked over them, they were a geological analysis of the rocks with veins of metal running through them. Mark spoke in a hurried and breathless voice, "Did you know that most metals still have trace elements of earth within them? It's from where they've been mined, even after they've been made into different alloys, the trace elements will remain, in most cases that is."

"Brilliant, Mark. But what's your point?"

"My point is, if the metals still have traces of earth within them, you, and others who can control earth, should be able to warp and control them in some way." I simply looked up at him, squinting in the somehow, overcast but bright light, clearly unconvinced. "Well, I suppose we won't know if we don't try." Desperation was beginning to seep into my head. Mark had been holding a small metal bannister rail, clearly just having been ripped off of his own boat, he handed it to me. The bar felt cold and unmoveable in my hands, but I persevered, willing the metal to move in some way. Nothing happened.

"Mark didn't you say that in the spirit world our powers are amplified? Can we take objects to that place? Maybe if I practised there, something might happen? I haven't even been actively using my powers for that long, this might just be a case of needing to learn more technique?"

"You know I've never actually tried to do that, suppose I've never really had the need to before now." Mark, took down his scarf from his face and rubbed his chin as he often did when in deep thought. He was now quite comfortable with me seeing his scarred face, and wore the scarf mostly out of habit, like a smoker who didn't really have the need to smoke any more, but just liked the feeling of it.

With a month to practice, we had mastered full body

transitions to the spirit world, to practice our powers and enjoy the extra space there. Without warning he grabbed my hand and before I could fully register what was happening. I was sucked inward to the pull of the transfer, my stone growing hot and glued to my hand, Marks words, "Come on then!" we were also dragged away by the force of the sudden change. Like being thrown off a playground toy I rocketed to the ground, exactly where we had left last time, like we had simply put our life there on pause.

I stood, slowly, my hair floating around my head in the thick air of that world. I put my hands on my knees willing vomit to come and put my stomach out of its misery. Mark stood tall and excited next to me, then noticed my strife, "Oh, sorry, forgot you're not used to that yet." He marched around looking for the metal pole I had been holding.

Once composed again, I was overtaken by the beauty of a land I could now visit whenever I chose, like a gigantic secret garden. Couldn't I just stay here, be a coward and forget how badly I had messed up in the real world? I sighed, I loved my friends and cared about the others too much for it not to drive me insane. Stupid feelings.

We were close to where Robyn had hidden her and Grace's stones, the hiding place proved useless as the stones glowed brightly as soon as I approached the shrub they had been hidden amongst. I smiled at the innocence of this place. It was almost childlike, the way it interacted with you. I picked up their stones from the ground, my brain was immediately confronted with their thoughts, like finally getting home after a long journey I drank in their voices and tears formed in my eyes as their faces popped into my head, our hive mind had connected for the first time in what felt like forever. In the background I could just about make out Mark getting frustrated about the metal pole, not being here with us. I tuned him out and dived into my friends' thoughts.

They were together with everyone else who had been on the island, and some new faces I didn't recognise. All of them crammed into what looked to be a shipping crate with horrible flickering lights above them, it looked cold and dirty, but somehow familiar. I realised it was Caroline's 'safety bunk' that had been brought in when wooden walls could no longer contain her.

From somewhere behind my friends a child cried. I could tell they had both realised I was once again with them, they covered their excitement well and stayed deathly quiet on the outside, but screeching with joy in their minds. "Well look who it is, talk about taking your time, ass hat," was my welcome from Grace. "Oh god, it's really you, well done! We knew you'd figure something out!"

Are you okay? Where are you? Are you close by, is that why you can hear us again?" was Robyn's frenzied response.

"I'm in the spirit world, I literally just picked up your stones, they were glowing. In the real world I'm nowhere near you. I've been staying with Mark trying to figure out how to get to you all, what can you tell me?" I was all business after the initial rush of hearing and seeing them again, I had to put my heart to one side and focus.

"They've had us in here for the entire time, Not gonna lie, it's been great not having to hear you witter on."

"Grace, I know you're happy to hear from me but you're in a lot of danger, and I need to get you out of there." I spoke as sternly as I could but with an undeniable grin on my face.

"All we know is this freaking box, I wish we could tell you more Millie, the only people we see are this bald-headed guy, one of the ones we were fighting by the lake, he takes one of us out every day at random." Robyn paused for a moment in her thoughts, deciding whether or not to tell me the rest to save my guilt.

"They don't come back." Grace finished for her. I swallowed hard. I needed more information.

"Are you still on the island?"

"They knocked us all out with those darts on that day, all me and Grace remember is waking up in here with everyone else. We do hear gulls every now and then though, so the assumption is that we're at least on the coast somewhere, or heaven forbid, near a bloody landfill."

"Nah, don't worry Mills, we hear them talking about the lab sometimes on the outside of our luxury new quarters, they'd be stupid to take Kit away from her kit, so to speak. I think we're definitely still on the island chick."

"Okay well, thanks for telling me all you know. Mark thinks we can work metal to our advantage, as you've both got time to kill, try to see if you can work that box you're in. I know it's a long shot, but it's all the help I can give you both right now—" I just saw Grace's face contort into serious doubt, while Robyn's looked up in alarm, they cut me off immediately.

My heart was still beating like a drum as I held their stones with mine, cradled in my hands, disconnected from them once again. I kept them all with me from then on. This form of communication outside of the limits of the hive mind would be essential to beating Kit at her game and getting everyone to safety. For the first time I felt like we had some sort of weapon over her growing empire of captivity.

I finally looked round to deal with Mark, still stropping over his plan having failed. He now sat by the river, plopping small rocks into it, their splashes exaggerated due to his stronger influence over air. As he was blocked out of our communications, I relayed everything to him, one hand on his back to comfort him. I couldn't think of how hard it must be to have your own mother as the person putting so many through so much pain and suffering. He was very quiet after, so I tried talking to him about the logistics of taking different items to the spirit world, and why it hadn't worked. I suggested we try to find some metal here instead. "No, there's no man-made stuff here, I've looked, this place seems to go on forever, but it's just nature and creatures, what use is that in this situation?" He shook his head as he spoke, I knew the feeling, exhaustion from thinking too hard, and yet still having no answers.

I sat on the round, river rocks with him and looked across the water. To my utter astonishment, there sat a small figure, cross-legged and smiling at us, not seven metres away. I hadn't heard anything approach and was quite alarmed. I pushed Mark hard on the arm, still staring open mouthed at the figure, who glowed like most things there. The being was smaller than most humans but perfectly proportioned, the face was strange and had a humanness about it, but somehow was very different to the average profile; smoother and more streamlined. The figure wore light-coloured robes, bell-shaped sleeves hiding its hands, folded in its lap.

We stared. Finally, it opened its eyes and spoke through its mind to us. An ethereal voice reached us, like several people speaking at once in a large cave.

"No evil can enter this place. That is why you struggle today. The enemy creates a master race. Hold your form, do not delay.

The help you need you already own. Unite your souls for a secret weapon.

The world will change we have always known.

This is fate, the futures beckon. The balance of life will always win. Good will be restored for all. Remember the answer lies within,

And you will live to see your foe's downfall."

The being made a small bow after this speech, and simply faded from sight altogether, leaving myself and Mark thunderstruck at what had just happened.

"Well, I guess that means metal is a no-no in the spirit world," Mark said, eyes still round from a mixture of fright and bewilderment.

Meanwhile my mind was already going at full speed, decoding the rhyme, I spoke aloud, "I think it must extend to most man-made objects here, I'm just thankful clothing seems to be acceptable by spirit standards."

"Amen to that."

"Nice to know you're right about your mother creating super soldiers though, that's one theory proved. We know time is of the essence already, don't need to be told that twice." I walked in circles now, listing off the points the poem had made using my fingers, "The help we need we already own, that's got to be a reference to the stone, or our powers, or both. It just can't be anything else."

"So I was right, we should just wing it and arrive on the island unprepared!"

"Shush, I'm thinking. 'Unite your souls for secret weapon', that's the most intriguing part, it must mean all of us with stones have to use them together, and unite our powers. When we do that something big's going to happen. Something that will allow us to beat Kit. Let's think, I'm the best at Earth, Grace has always been great with water and Robyn with air. You're brilliant with fire. All of us have stones…" In the air in front of me, like my thoughts had transgressed into physical things, the four symbols for the elements presented themselves in bright, silvery lines as if written by hand. The four were spaced out as if in a square formation, then thin lines connected them, one by one making the shape of a star. Only the star had five points, the topmost point was blank for a few seconds, then instead of a triangle marking like the other elements a small, perfect circle showed itself there. I had no idea what power this represented, but it was almost definitely what would be released with all four of our powers and stones united.

I stared at Mark, with absolute delight. He no longer looked down and dejected, he once again had the spark and hope in his eyes I liked so much. "The best part is I think we'll definitely beat her! 'The balance of life will always win', right? Nothing can go wrong!" I envied his optimism, the balance of life didn't necessarily mean no one would die. It's a balance after all.

Decoy Whale

The weather over the next few weeks was set to be perfect for sailing, we both agreed there was simply no point in waiting any longer, and I begrudgingly admitted that we should just 'wing it' as Mark had so eloquently put days earlier.

We were roughly a four-day trip away from the island, as Mark adjusted various complex ropes and strips of canvas to propel us forward, I thought of our eventual approach to Living Stone Island. I discussed with him a technique of using our powers to travel underwater on the last leg of the journey, still keeping his boat behind the cliffs at a distance from the island. A combined effort of my power over water and his over air would mean we could literally create an underwater sphere to travel in undetected. Mark would need to stay very close to me the closer we got, as I was the only thing keeping him from being detected by his mother's shark-like senses, according to him.

I was pleased to find out that Mark was a strong swimmer, so if our plan did happen to go down like a sack of bricks, he would at least have a chance of surviving it. In the two days it took to sail there we took several breaks in the daylight to practice my new idea. The waters were getting quite warm so it wasn't an unpleasant experience even when our 'bubble' burst. First, I would get in the water, making as big a pit around myself, keeping the sea away from me whilst I simultaneously tread water, Mark would then jump in beside me and create his air orb around us. We found this much easier to do on the surface, as we tried to go deeper for what would be more coverage from Kit's look-out that would no doubt be littered all over the island, we found it increasingly difficult to master. The water's pressure would get too much just as we got deep enough not to be seen from the surface, Mark would slip first and it would be down to me to keep us from drowning whilst we swam to the surface, sometimes only just making it and gasping for air, always finding ourselves a mile or two from the safety of the boat as well.

On the last day of travelling a shoal of mackerel was darting about playfully around us as we tried, yet again to master our bubble. They swam in such numbers, so dense they blacked out the sky seen above us from the sea. An idea struck me, "Mark! The fish, the bloody fish! We're saved!"

"I don't know about you, but I'm still full from breakfast."

"No, you idiot, we can influence animals too, can't we? What if we had the fish hide us from above? We'd be completely hidden from Kit, visually and from heat sensing monitors!"

"You know, sometimes I wonder if we're really the best people to be doing this, maybe it's the sun getting to us, why on earth didn't we think of this before now?" Mark sighed in happy exasperation. Laughing we both extended out our hive minds to the mackerel, which were still circling us, as if they were already planning on helping anyway. Without much fight, we had them completely cover us in under an hour.

On the last leg of the journey, Mark steered the boat and I focused all my energies in keeping the school of fish with us, if they left, we were doomed, only they didn't leave, in fact more and more came, to the point where we had a comical amount of sea life around out boat at all times. I spoke to the ocean, and its creatures heard my call of distress. By the end of the last day in the boat we had not just the mackerel, but about a dozen dolphins, several groupings of red mullet, pollack and cod and even a monstrous humpback whale and its calf. Mark was confident this was simply too much and our disguise was quickly turning into a clear alarm signal for the enemy island inhabitants. I agreed, but now I had called them, they wouldn't leave. I hoped too much was better than not enough, for our sakes and the fish, or mammals as Mark repeatedly corrected me about the dolphins and whales.

Eventually, after a restless night's sleep in the rocking boat, repeatedly being bumped by the sea life beneath it, myself and Mark gave up on sleep and decided a post sunrise rescue was in order. We donned the wetsuits, mine was the only one with zip-able pockets, I took both of our stones for safekeeping. The wetsuits were cold and still soaking from the day before, we jumped in. There is nothing liked chilled seawater to force you into wakefulness.

The fish jumped out of the water in — supposed, by me and Mark — eagerness to help. I couldn't help feeling more confident and positive with a bottlenose dolphin squeaking and crackling right at me in the post sunrise light. Mark looked at me, grinned, and gave me the nod. It was time.

Like a well-orchestrated musical number, we all swam in unison, away from Mark's boat, docked just out of sight from the still very far away island. Our bubble was stronger with our increased confidence. Not to mention a humongous whale beneath us and hundreds of creatures above us, it felt like we had a whole army charging forth in the water, and like the fight was a little more equalised.

As we slowly crept closer though, my stomach dropped; all around the sea in front of us were strong beams of light, piercing through the water. Search lights, even with our camouflage they still might catch a glimpse of us with those. Closer still and we started to see great, dark, elongated shapes breaking the water's surface, I realised they were large ships. I didn't want to think what was waiting for us on the decks of those monsters. "Probably more monsters," replied Mark in my head. We needed a large distraction, I reached out only to the humpback whale this time, through my mind I asked it to make a scene away from us. It complied immediately and we heard its graceful splashes and felt the vibrations of its jumps from our bubble. Mark gave me an impressed thumbs up, we were too tired with swimming now to chit chat. No one, not even on guard lookouts can resist looking at that kind of spectacle of nature. You can always rely on whales to mesmerise, and distract.

My plan must have worked as we were now right up close to the large ships docked near the island, and still hadn't been spotted. Once past, I tried connecting with Grace and Robyn to get their location, holding my stone carefully in my zippy wetsuit pocket. Robyn answered immediately, not even taking the time to greet me all I got was, "South west corner of the island near the cottage, hurry!" Before she cut me off. There must have been a reason for this, either they could now detect out communication or she was in serious trouble and needed all her concentration, or both. I looked at Mark, panic rising in my chest, the fish around us picking up on it and swimming frantically around us. We had no plan from here on, I silently cursed Mark and the strange being in the spirit world. Great idea this. Fab.

Suddenly Mark turned to me, eyes round as golf balls and gestured with his hands making silly circlets and shapes with them against the rocks of the island, we were now swimming alongside. He furiously pointed at me and then again at the rocks. Slowly, like ice melting, I got what he meant; we had to tunnel through the rock and core of the island. Mark was running out of energy fast, I had to work quickly, I hoped to high heaven that I would crush us both with my lack of tunnel making knowledge, at least this way we would be able to breathe though.

I let my fear and panic for my friends fuel my fight against the hard, marbled rocks underwater. It was like trying to take a leisurely sip of thick treacle compared to how easy it was obliterating stone above water. My heart pumped faster forcing the adrenaline through my veins, I had no other option, it was this or everyone gets captured, I wasn't even sure if our whale was still putting on a show, we could have been found out at any time. It took all my will and inner force to pummel through those first few rocks, of course whatever progress I had made was filled with water, up and up I went, Mark's air bubble getting ever smaller. At about twelve foots progress, the water breached and I held my head above the water line choking and heaving, Mark's air bubble having been diminished for about a minute, having to make two holding spots for myself and Mark to limply grip on to while we caught our breath.

"We freaking made it!" Mark whisper-shouted at me, face dripping with water.

"Not yet we haven't, still have to try and reach the cottage with a terrible sense of direction through these bloody great rocks." To save the effort of pointing I simply rolled my eyes around our surrounds to indicate the work that still needed to be done.

"Best hop to it then, Mills, come on make a room for us to dry off in and them we can get going again". The stone above us was made of something slightly softer than the base rocks underwater, so was easier for me to manoeuvre. Once we could stand up in our room, Mark shot a fire to life in the middle and used his own conjured flames in his hands to dry himself off. I copied and found it was surprisingly easy, never would I ever be cold again.

Once warm and dry, and above all, not shivering violently, it was almost a pleasant process gradually chipping away at the rocks, roughly westwards to our best estimation. Every now and then I would hit a particularly soft vein of clay or crumbly rocks and travel it as far as I dared, Mark using his air ability to sweep away the dust and dirt from our breathing space.

At one point we got too close to the edge, an almost heart shattering moment arrived when I mindlessly cracked through a large particularly stubborn rock only to find daylight had come and was streaming in through a dinner plate sized hole I'd made. Without thinking I covered it instantly with clay from out feet. Panting, I asked, "Do you think anyone saw us?" A few seconds later we both looked up as an ear-splitting siren started to howl on the ground above us.

"Maybe," Mark said.

Rescue Mission

Without having time to talk it through I made a huge chasm above us and Mark lifted us up with his air bubble. I sealed the tunnel below us and we dug faster than ever trying to make a significant gap between the hole in the cliff where they'd seen us. Mark covered our tracks, pushing the rocks I crumbled back into the shaft behind us and lighting our way with small floating orbs of fire. We could now hear the aircraft chopping in the air not five feet away from us, if they couldn't use Kit's sense to find us, they would sure be able to use infrared, no longer were we covered by a mass of fish to protect us from them seeing our tell-tale heat blotches against the cool rock we carved through. To make matters worse the next few armfuls of rock I dug through revealed a corrugated metal plate, I fruitlessly dug along it for a metre or so but the metal sheet was so large we ended up quite trapped.

"Millie, the metal!"

"Yes, I can see that, we're screwed."

"No, I think that's where everyone is, they said they were in a metal container right?" I looked at Mark, wide-eyed for a split second before, wildly banging on the metal with my fists, not bothering to be quiet any more, we were found out now for sure, what was the point in trying to keep it down? Mark helpfully handed me a sizeable chunk of stone to make a bigger impact. I screamed for my friends banging the rock, while close behind us we heard the tell-tale booms and thuds of minor explosives eating away at our small wall of protection, "ROBYN, GRACE,

ANYONE?" Dust fell in my eyes but I screamed louder still, I hadn't come this far to be a failure. The muffled sounds of voices from the other side of the metal sounded, scrabbling noises of what sounded like large furniture being moved were heard, and then a loud, clunking, ripping of metal. The stones grew kettle hot in my pocket and I knew they were in there, just as desperate as us.

Mark suddenly motioned for us to swap places, I needed to hold off the people with explosives behind us while we opened the metal sheet. I tried a different tack; instead of building up a thicker wall, I blasted through, taking the three men in dark camo uniforms by surprise, knocking them to the floor with the force of rock and dirt that fell upon them. My adrenaline surged as I swept the unconscious bodies out of the hole in the cliff in one fell swoop, my patience was at its limit. If they wouldn't play fair, then neither would I. Sealing up the holes after I turned again to Mark who was blasting the metal with an unholy amount of heat, what was emitting from his hands was not red but blue in colour, I'd never seen him produce fire like that before, but it was working the metal bent and warped far easier for the people inside the container, I joined in giving everything I had in me to try to force the sheet back up on itself. There must have been about seven people working it, but together with our combined power, the metal finally broke away to reveal a two foot hole, just big enough to clamber through. I smiled a sweaty grin at Mark, he had been right about being able to work with metal after all, it just took more than one of us. He was visibly thrilled about it, even in the circumstances.

Mark wasted little time and grabbed me by the hips, hoisting me up to the hands offering to help us up out of the ground, we gingerly avoided the still searing hot jagged metal. Once up I helped him through and sealed the entrance with rock, even knowing it wouldn't last long. At last, I looked around our new surroundings, my eyes locked on Robyn and Grace; both looked overjoyed to see me, but were also drawn and thin, Grace in particular looked as if she'd lost about a third of her body weight. They were as grimy and dusty as myself and Mark as well, and they hadn't even been making a tunnel underground all morning.

Silent tears made great creeks in the dust that covered our faces as we all stood together in a strange, three-way hug. Over their heaving shoulders I saw the familiar faces of everyone I had known on the island; the children huddled together in a corner, Angela and some of the other older women crowded around them, Chunhua and her friends standing together conversing in lightning-fast mandarin, even Gus was in here, sitting against the wall, arms on his knees stretched outwards, quite relaxed, as if this was a normal way of life, stuck in a windowless shipping container, held prisoner.

I reached into my pocket and retrieved their stones, still white hot, and said simply, "Go now." Grace nodded like this was the plan all along and grabbed a still spluttering Robyn and made the transformation to the spirit world herself, dragging her along. There wasn't time for everyone else to react to two people completely disappearing before the large floor to ceiling doors were swung open and two armed guards with giant shiny black boots came swaddling in. Everyone immediately got into lines as if this was routine and sat crossed legged on the filthy floor. Mark grabbed me and pulled me to the floor just in time. One of the men started performing a head count. I realised with two new arrivals and with two just departed, if this thug hadn't bothered to memorise everyone's faces, we were in the clear. At least for now.

"Pah, forty-six, same as before, dunno what that woman's on about 'alf the time Dave. Bleedin' paranoid if you ask me."

"Huh, yeah, perhaps if she stopped list-ning to that machine o' hers that don't do her no good she wouldn't fink a strong breeze meant intruders were comin'."

"Ohhhhh, the waves are big today, best do double shifts!"

"Ahhhhh the birds are flying counter clockwise, no pay fur anyone fura week!"

"Hurhurhur, good one, Dave."

"Thanks Dave."

Whilst Dave and Dave were chit-chatting Mark slunk into the shadows of the shipping container, unnoticed by both guards. By the time they had finished their banter Mark was on the other side of the doors, Dave and Dave turned around to find themselves face to face with Mark's signature smirk, before they both received a heavy thud from both of the metal doors, and promptly fell to the ground, mouths still agape.

I scurried over to help Mark drag the unconscious bodies back into the shipping container and close up the doors again. I looked as Mark frantically started undressing the smaller of the Daves, chucking his enormous boots to the side saying, "Those will never fit you, best stick with what you've got on." I looked to my feet, black river shoes, still squelching with sea water. At least they were dark.

"So I take it the plan is to play dress up?" I enquired after a minute or so of helping to undress the Daves.

"Well, unless you've got a better idea, yeah. I was thinking we could look the part as we march this lot to the docks and hopefully get them into a boat without anyone noticing."

"You realise just how unlikely that is, right?"

"Yup."

"Good, just checking."

I turned to the frightened-looking inhabitants of the island, whilst dressing over the top of my wetsuit. They looked hopeful, because of me and scared because of Mark, I realised they were probably still under the impression he was a murderer. I looked for Caroline to explain, but she wasn't there. "They've taken her," a chorus of voices in my head from the crowd. I cottoned on and showed them my memory of Mark's expatiation of what happened that day. I saw shoulders ease and foreheads increase afterwards. This made all the more sense for them in their situation, Kit definitely was the bad guy there, it didn't take much to convince them.

"Okay now that's all cleared up, we have no time to lose, I need information of the best route to get you guys off the island." I sounded much more confident and authoritative than I felt, I needed this to go well. Half of a good plan is confidence, after all.

At that point Gus stood and communicated through the hive mind to everyone, out of necessity rather than anything else, not everyone understood sign language, "I hear their break alarm going at midday, but they swap shifts an hour before, your best bet is to wait ten minutes for the switch, at that point we'll have a few seconds to all run out. After that all we can hope for is that there's an unoccupied boat down on the shore some place, 'cause mine never came back." Gus eyed me with intense reverence for a moment, and a wash of guilt came over me. Drat. So he'd noticed that minor hiccup when myself, Grace and Robyn took his sail boat...

"Surely we'd have a better chance if we weren't in such a large group? Why don't we go in smaller groups or even pairs?" Angela suggested.

"The size of the group doesn't matter when Millie is with you, you're all covered by her wavelength right now, the moment she leaves you outside of this box, sensors will go off notifying Kit where you are. Millie cancels out the tracking senses my mother has, it's our only chance of getting off the island unnoticed. We have to stick together." Mark spoke loudly, but with a sombre tone, knowing how frustrating the situation was for everyone. They may have been covered by my wavelength, but we were still an unmissable and sizeable group of people. I coughed awkwardly with so many people staring at me.

I realised it was nearly time for the switch-over, a time where guards were walking from one place to another, slightly less focused on patrols than usual, we had to go now. My throat was dry and the smallest of the two Daves' clothing was making me itch and sweat. I swallowed hard and asked Gus to lead the way as myself and Mark stood with the Daves' guns just outside of the container, trying our best to look as if this was us just following orders from higher up. One by one people left, all of them squinting in the sunlight, I wondered how long it had been since they had all seen the light of day. Mark ordered the team to halt in a voice incredibly similar to whom we were impersonating, I silently congratulated him on his voice over skills while I locked the container and took the key with me. I was hoping the next set of guards would just assume it was a mix up and find another key, but any hold up, no matter how short was valuable to us.

Gus led the group at a fast paced walk down the cliffside steps, we couldn't run as that would draw even more attention. We had a few looks from other guards travelling to their next locations, Mark was a natural and gave them all a quick, jerking nod as if he was too busy to talk right now. This confidence saved us on three occasions. I simply looked forward my cap dipped low over my eyes, with a stern face.

The group's heartbeats grew faster as we were on the final approach to the main docking point of the island. Mark called the group to a stop again and broke off to coerce the guards by the boats. They looked like rookies, two barely adult boys stood with light hair and a matching set of angry, red acne on their faces. Standing facing the island with my gun held up I could hear him impatiently telling rookie guard number one that his orders were from 'the boss' and 'if they didn't hurry up and find them a boat, he'd personally make sure they were fired'. The spotty pair of young guards spoke of protocol and authenticity codes we needed to have Mark's voice never wavered in his persuasion.

He tried a different tack, looking at their name badges, "Ahh well this explains it, Jacobs," He held up their scanning machines, ready and waiting for the codes we didn't have to cross the harbour barrier. "No one's told you, have they?"

"Told us what sir?"

"The machine's boys, they're out for today, some maggot, more dim-witted than yourselves, broke them yesterday, you may as well have been scanning bananas all damned day, AHAHAHA!" Mark hollered while chucking the machine back into their pathetically small 'office' on the docks. The boys looked at each other.

"You know I did think it was odd that Corporal Mayfair's didn't glitch like it usually does today," spoke one of the boys.

"Not to worry lads, I won't hold it against you both, today. But if this happens again you can be sure I'll be reporting you for incompetence, understand?"

"Sir, yes sir!" They both made elaborate salutes and let the group pass one by one, Mark simply standing by the door of one of the many identical boats with his gun at the ready, somehow, he'd even found a toothpick to chew on. He was enjoying this far too much.

As the last islander was on the boat and myself and Mark, were hastily undoing the boats' ropes, knowing all it would take was one person to notice, we'd already pushed our luck considerably, it surely was running out now. Mark gave the boat a great push and jumped on, and then turned around holding out his hand for me to join, I saw his eyes grow large when he turned to face me. I felt a bony, ring filled hand clutch my shoulder, "You know it's not every day that a whole batch of test subjects just pops off the radar in an instant. It's funny how your main advantage against me is what actually gave you away. Isn't it Millie?"

Battle

With one fluid motion Kit raised her other hand, churning the waters around the boat, bringing it back to the shore, Mark fought back with the power of wind, knocking Kit to the floor, people spilled out of the boats' doorway fighting with him. Kit pressed a button and a communications device on her shirt and hundreds of soldiers came running down to the beach. My stone grew hot in my pocket once more, I did the only thing I could and held Kit by the arm as I transformed us to the spirit world.

Kit's face contorted in astonishment as we travelled, landing in an open plain seconds later in the strange white-washed world where the air was thicker and every motion easier. We both gradually got up from the floor panting, waiting for the other to make a move. "You stupid girl. You can never win against me. I am far too powerful and far too wise to fall for your tricks."

"This is no trick, Kit, this place is real."

"Nonsense." She was mesmerised by the sheer beauty of her new world, and decided I wasn't enough of a threat to risk wandering for a moment. We were near a cliff side that fell many metres down to an ocean. A waterfall was close by, falling into the depths. Quickly, she realised that her powers were far stronger here, finding the waterfall and making the stream flow upwards in a grand movement, then letting it fall once more.

"Well, this is all quite incredible, but it doesn't really solve our little problem does it?" Kit spoke softly as her hair waved around her shoulders, suspended in the thick atmosphere. She turned to me and without warning made a giant chasm exactly where I had been standing. I turned and grabbed on to the ledge of the split earth, wondering for the first time if I could even die in this place. Kit smiled at my struggle but I sent a roaring flame of fire along her line of destruction, the flames blew up when they hit the end at her feet and engulfed her in fire. This only made her adrenaline rush and powered her to make even more drastic manoeuvres; when I made large chunks of rock fly at her she easily made a wall to protect herself in time from the ground up, when I used the river behind her to trip her up she got higher still. Atop her small mountain I used air to whisk her off and she fell, properly damaged for the first time.

I walked over to her, despite all her wrongdoings not wanting her to be dead. Like an opossum she had only played dead and grabbed my ankles, sealing them to the ground with rock. I only just dodged the fire ball she threw at me by cracking the earth beneath myself so that I fell instead of burned. Clinging onto the rocks once more she strode over to me, crushing my fingers with her boot as she spoke, "Why don't you just give it up? You really don't stand a chance, why waste your time? You can come with me, I'll give you all the protection you want, I promise I'll forgive and forget, this place would be very useful to learn about in my field of expertise. What do you say? Friends?" Kit held out a hand to me, I yanked it and pulled her down with me, I had been standing quite steady on the ledge I had made, two could play at the fake game. Kit fell through the air for some time before I caught her with an air bubble, she could only change the earth and waters around her as long as I kept her far enough away from those things, I was safe.

I climbed back up the ledge, all the while holding her in my self-made mini prison. I took the opportunity to catch my breath. Holding her as high as I could, hearing only muffled screeches from her. Then I saw them; Grace and Robyn using their stones just inside the tree line on the edge of the rocky plain we had been fighting in. They both half-ran over to me, "These things are handy, aren't they? Did you know they kind of act like a beacon to each other too? They get warmer the closer you get!" Grace exclaimed, thrilled.

"That's how I found you two on the island."

"But I gave you directions!"

"Yeah, not so great when you're underground and have no idea which way is north, you pudding." I laughed at Robyn. But Robyn's retorted smiled faded, she was looking upwards. I turned and saw that Kit had somehow managed to gather water from the air around her and was making a huge mass around her, the shadow of it encompassing almost the entire plain, the size of a football field. She dropped the mass of water right on top of us. Momentarily submerged in the new lake that Kit had essentially created I saw both my friends struggle in the water beside me, they were weak from not using their powers in so long and were struggling to even swim. Under the water I gestured for them to retreat, giving an 'okay' sign with my fingers. I had a plan. Swimming to the bottom of the plain, I grabbed their stones and held them in my hand with mine and Marks. The spirit creatures' words drifted back into my mind; 'The help you need you already own.' I held all four stones tightly and felt the power of not just the stones, but of my love for my friends, the power of nature and my own force inside my soul surged outwards.

I burst out of the water, my whole body glowing a bright and radiant blue. The light shone out of my chest like the sun itself. No thoughts came, every action was as easy and as natural as the coming of the tides. I matched Kit's level up in the air and a burst like a gamma ray rang through me, blasting Kit back to the ground like a rag doll. I gently soared down to meet her, and held out the four stones in front of her, channelling their energy straight into her chest. The light around me grew bigger and brighter and a strange substance came from Kit, pooling in the air just above where her body lay. A darkness. It looked rotten and fowl. Her body rose up slightly, as if possessed, as this strange inky mass came out of her, her eyes rolled and all that could be seen were the whites, she shook for a moment and then the darkness was blasted out of sight by the rocks I held up. My own body came back to itself. I dropped to my knees on the still wet plain, puddles forming around where Kit lay, motionless on the ground.

I held her body and wept. I had never wanted her to die. Her marks on her right arm started to swirl upon her skin, and eventually faded into nothing. As I crouched there, crying miserably, the spirit creature appeared once more; its mere presence was enough to calm me. Crossed legged like before, it communicated through the hive mind,

"Everyone deserves a second chance. Do not fear, her life does remain.

She will not remember her former stance.

Or the evil, blood and pain.

You followed my advice. You have done so very well. The woman has paid the price. Now she lives in an empty shell.

You have proven worth and courage. We have given you the power to hold. With your help the world can flourish. You must teach them, young and old.

Your land is changing day by day.

Less anger, sloth and wrath. What the future holds, no one can say. Time will choose the smoothest path."

And with that the spirit faded once more. I felt my friends' hands on my shoulders and Kit stirred. We travelled back, before she saw the world she had nearly conquered.

Journey's End

In the weeks that flew by, I started noticing more and more crispy leaves, bundled up into corners from cold winds. Autumn was coming soon. The island was just starting to feel like home again.

The navel boats and helicopters left with the aid of the fifth element I had unlocked in the spirit world. All that was needed was a gathered assembly of the squadrons that had arrived, I held the stones like I had with Kit in front of a huge assembly of people clad in army gear, like swarms of bees they silently gathered up their gear and left without question. Mark, always the cautious one, made some investigations, there was apparently no evidence of anything notable on their records of Living Stone Island. Everyone simply forgot. We were left in peace.

We remained undecided on what to do with Kit. Like a child she looked at the island upon returning with new eyes. She couldn't even remember where she had lived for so many years. Let alone who Mark was. A number of individuals suggested she be allowed to stay, as she was no longer a threat, but this proved to leave a bad taste in Mark's mouth, so after a month she was taken to the mainland to live in sheltered accommodation, with carers on site twenty-four seven. She seemed oblivious to her circumstances, and happy enough there. The people at the home helped Mark with power of attorney and the island was changed to his ownership, as the only living heir of his family's wealth. Kit's lack of memory was put down to early onset dementia.

From then on Mark took control of the island, much of Kit's regime was kept; the daily job lists and meal times and lessons continued. The only difference really was that there were strictly no experiments allowed. Kit's lab lay abandoned, for good. That and the fact that everyone felt it suddenly okay to see their families once more, insisting that they had found work on an eco-farm and were staying for a while. The story was generally believed, even by the most sceptical of friends and families.

Myself and Mark talked on many nights of what would happen to the increasing number of people discovering that they had powers. With no Kit to sense them out, who would make sure they had somewhere safe to learn about their powers? For weeks no one new showed, but with the new relaxed attitude of the island, people started to go back to their families to visit. The hive mind we discovered could do more than allow us to communicate; Robyn came back from seeing her family one day with her two brothers and their father in the boat with her. Whilst on a walk one day they had heard her thoughts and followed the familiar warmth of someone like them. Robyn was overjoyed to teach her siblings herself, and regain her family once more. More and more incidents like this happened, soon people from all over the globe inhabited the island. The hive mind spread and stretched as we travelled to different and more distant places.

Chunhua, as one of the most competent of the island, decided to start up another retreat for people like us in her home country. Her grandfather had land high up in the mountains of China where another colony would be safe. A new era for people like us had seemingly arrived, a happier and healthier one. One without fear.

Like I said at the beginning of this story, I still have no idea if what we are doing is the right thing. All I know is that to follow the path of your destiny is something you must do, even if you leave behind, people that you love. For when you truly want something, with all your being, the world works with you, in ways that aren't perceptible at first, but if you stand still and quiet, and listen to the world around you signs are everywhere. They can help you find your true meaning in life.

Stop and wait at the river and see the way the leaves move as they land on the water. Sense the rain coming. Feel the dust on the hottest day of summer. Notice the sway of the beech trees on those first windy days of the year. It is different for everyone, but everyone can do it. Listen to the soul and heartbeat of your own world.

What will I do now my journey is through? I'm not sure, I'll probably keep listening, waiting for the next signs. All I know is that the wind still blows, fires still roar, the waves still leave spray on the mighty rocks of the land. I know I am still here, still following my own path. Still.